THE
PITCHFORK
REVIEW

Contents

Features

Toons

Photo

Control P

SUBSCRIBING IS LIKE FOLLOWING US ON TUMBLR, ONLY THICKER AND MORE EXPENSIVE.

THE PITCHFORK REVIEW

THE PITCHFORK REVIEW Nº. 1 2013

ISSUE 1 MASTHEAD ILLUSTRATION BY TIM LAHAN

Ryan Schreiber
FOUNDER AND CEO

Christopher Kaskie
PRESIDENT AND PUBLISHER

Michael Renaud
CREATIVE DIRECTOR

J.C. Gabel
EDITOR AND ASSOCIATE PUBLISHER

Editorial

Mark Richardson
*Contributing Editor &
Editor-in-Chief of
Pitchfork.com*

Ryan Dombal
Contributing Editor

Megan Frestedt
Jessica Hundley
Sybil Perez
Sam Sweet
Rachel Wiseman
Copy Editors

Contributing Writers

Carrie Battan
Larry Fitzmaurice
Robert Gordon
Jayson Greene
Jessica Hundley
Mimi Lipson
Chris Molanphy
Mike Powell
Peter Relic
Simon Reynolds
Amanda Petrusich
Nick Sylvester
Lindsay Zoladz

Illustrations, Photography, and Artwork

Se Young Au, Erez Avissar, Michael DeForge,
Nabil Elderkin, Sophie Goldstein, Paul
Hornschemeier, Simon Hanselmann, Patch
Keyes, Tim Lahan, Hannah K. Lee, Brandon
Loving, Jeaneen Lund, James McShane, Niall
O'Brien, Ron Regé, Jr., Kyle Dean Reinford,
Johnny Sampson, Sterling Texas, Tonje Thilesen

Colophon

Set in Tiempos Text & Display from Klim Type
Foundry (*klim.co.nz*), the Circular family from
Lineto (*lineto.com*), Lydia from the Colophon
Foundry (*colophon-foundry.or*g), and GT Haptik
from Grilli Type (*grillitype.com*). Printed on
Finch Fine bright white antique 70# text,
porcelainECO 30 gloss100# text, and Mohawk
Superfine white eggshell 80# text. Cover is
printed on Sappi McCoy silk 100# cover.

Art and Development

Joy Burke
Molly Butterfoss
Graphic Design

Erik Sanchez
Photo Editor

Matthew Dennewitz
VP, Technology

Mark Beasley
Andrew Gaerig
Neil Wargo
Developers

Business & Operations

RJ Bentler
VP, Video Programming

Matthew Frampton
VP, Business

Megan Davey
VP, Finance

Megan Frestedt
Logistics

Ashley MaGee
Ash Slater
Brandon Stosuy
Events & Support

Welcome to *The Pitchfork Review.*

What you have in your hands is the inaugural issue of Pitchfork's print quarterly. After 17 years online, we thought it was finally time to bring you something you can hold. Since so much of enjoying music has to do with real, physical interactions—from going to shows to playing records—why not read about music culture in the same way?

We love the speed and community of the internet, but there's so much noise (and far too few filters) that important stories can get lost. We work hard on what we publish day-to-day, and put so much of ourselves into the features we run on Pitchfork.com. We wanted an opportunity to give some pieces a second life, one that won't be lost to Google searches and Twitter archives. And we also think this format is the perfect environment for presenting new writing and visual content that stands the test of time. This publication features contributions by some of today's finest writers, illustrators, and photographers. Their work should be studied, considered, and enjoyed, not deleted. Their subject, in the pages of *The Pitchfork Review*, is music culture.

We encourage you to set this issue down, get up and get a cup of coffee or tea, and come back to it, later on. We want you to take it with you on the train or to the beach. Eventually, we want you to place it on your bookshelf, perhaps lend it to your friends, tear out its pages, and (maybe) one day pass it on to your children as a time capsule of sorts, reflecting a four-month chunk of time in the 21st century.

—Pitchfork

WORTH

BY

SIMON

REYNOLDS

THEIR

In an era of instant access

everything, one writer recollects the

UK weekly music press of yore.

ILLUSTRATIONS BY JAMES MCSHANE

WAIT

Imagine, if you can, or remember, if you're old enough, a long-ago time when music fans had to wait. Wait for news about music. Wait for reviews that were really previews of music you'd wait even longer to hear. (No teasing tasters, sanctioned streams, or illicit leaks in those days.) Anticipation and delay structured the daily experience of music fandom in the pre-internet era. All music and most information were things you literally got your hands on: they came only in analogue form, as tangible objects like records or magazines.

In Britain, where I grew up, the primary source of news, commentary, and critique was the weekly music press: *New Musical Express*, *Melody Maker*, *Sounds*, and *Record Mirror*. The weeklies were stubbornly solid, slightly grubby things. Nicknamed "inkies" because their pages stained your fingers, they were printed on paper and shipped physically across the country, and also, in smaller quantities and at a more expensive price, to far-flung territories of the globe. How's this for anticipation and delay? In those days *NME* and the other papers reached Australia and New Zealand by surface mail and thus arrived several months after they came out in the UK, by which time the British scene would have moved forward a considerable distance.

At a time when pop coverage in mainstream newspapers was sporadic and detached-sounding, and TV even more intermittent, *NME, MM, Sounds,* and *RM* were the music fan's mainline to the rock world. People growing up in America in the 1970s got a similarly electric feeling of connection through magazines like *Creem*, a monthly, or *Rolling Stone*, published every two weeks. But because they came out 51 times a year (the Christmas issue was a double that lasted for a fortnight) rather than 12 or 26 times, the UK music papers created a far more immersive feeling, as if there was a rock reality running parallel to the official world of current affairs and mainstream

entertainment. The momentousness and urgency transmitted by the inkies in their prime was totally involving. Wednesday was the most exciting day of the week for the UK music fiend: that was when the papers arrived in the shops. Tuesday, if you lived in London and trekked to one of a handful of newspaper kiosks in the city center that sold hot-off-the-press publications, but for most of the country, Wednesday. Like tens of thousands of other young people, I would dash down to my local W.H. Smith, the big national chain of "newsagents" (along with newspapers and mags, it also sold books, stationery, and records). Since funds were limited and vinyl competed as a priority, I would buy one magazine loyally (*NME*) but stand there in the store flicking through the other three, speed reading as much of the content salient to my concerns as I could before the staff got cross. So in any given week, that would involve gauging the spectrum of opinion on a major release (the new Ian Dury, Joy Division's *Closer*), checking what was Single of the Week in each paper, and rapid-scanning interviews with figures I found compelling, like PiL's Jah Wobble or Scritti Politti's Green Gartside. [1]

At its peak of sales, approximately 1976 to 1981, the combined circulation of the British rock press was around half a million. But its actual readership was much larger, albeit impossible to quantify precisely. Paul Rambali, a former *NME* staff member, told me that the paper's pass on rate was 10 pairs of eyes for every copy sold, which would equate to a readership that fluctuated between two and two-and-a-half million during the postpunk era. As many as one out of every 22 people in the UK at that time. That sounds a little overblown to me, but the fact that this is how Rambali *remembers* it in itself speaks to the power of the *NME* and, to a lesser extent, *Sounds* and *Melody Maker*.

With hardly any serious competition (beyond a few, minority interest monthlies and some desultory cover-

[1] Elsewhere in Britain, many people accessed the rock press via an institution called the sixth-form common room. Equivalent to grades eleven and twelve in high school, sixth form comprised pupils being streamed for university. Some sixth-formers were given positions of responsibility, as prefects. Another privilege of seniority was the common room, basically a space for hanging out with your peers. Sixth-form common rooms often subscribed to one or more of the music papers. This contributed to the weekly music press's unusually high "pass on" rate, the magazine industry's term for the average number of people who read each purchased copy.

age in the newspapers), the weekly rock papers enjoyed a captive readership. They were practically the sole source of news, interviews, and in-depth critical analysis for rock and its adjacent genres. And because the record industry and live music promoters relied on the inkies to reach their target market with news of upcoming albums or tours, the music papers were flush with advertising revenue. This had two major effects. Because the number of editorial pages was in direct proportion to the number of ad pages, the papers' near-monopoly on music industry advertising allowed a huge amount of space for writing. Some issues ran over 100 pages. The ad revenue also served to make the papers highly profitable, which encouraged the media conglomerates that owned them (IPC, Morgan Grampian, United Newspapers, and EMAP) to avoid meddling in the affairs of editorial staffs.

Free from top-down interference, financially buoyant, loyally supported by a huge readership looking to be guided and enlightened, and covering a beat that was the indisputable center of contemporary culture, but also a prism through which one could examine politics or other art forms like film and fiction, the British rock press understandably developed a healthy collective ego—to put it mildly. This self-belief, which applied to each paper on the institutional level but also endowed certain individual writers with a messianic streak, was a self-fulfilling confidence trick. Act like you have the power to steer music in a righteous direction and you can make others believe; soon enough you *are* steering it. That was what some, if by no means all, of the inkie readership looked to the papers for: not just documentation or diagnosis, but a sense of where the music was

going and what its possibilities were. To follow this unfolding teleology, this evolutionary dialectic of swerve and counter-reaction, through the pages of the weeklies, was a thrilling ride.

Back in those days, I didn't know anything about the infrastructural background of the music press's megalomania, but I definitely picked up on the tone, the aura of conviction and certainty. The first one I bought, aged 16, was *Melody Maker*. In June 1979, I was in W.H. Smith and spotted the impish face of Malcolm McLaren on a lower shelf. Through my much more street-credible younger brother Tim, I'd heard things like Sex Pistols, Ian Dury, X-Ray Spex, and Buzzcocks. So I bought that issue of *MM* and found inside the final installment of a three-part profile of the former Pistols manager written by staff writer Michael Watts that doubled as a kind of requiem for punk. The piece was excellently written and highly informative, although I was puzzled initially by references to the Situationists. (Who were they? They sound like the most subversive, destructive rock band ever! Must get the records!). I probably reread that article half a dozen times over that summer.

Then in the autumn term of 1979, I began reading the *NME*. To say that this paper had a formative influence on me would be a typically English understatement. Pretty much all my expectations of what music writing could be, and should be, were shaped by exposure to *NME* as an impressionable and hugely impressed youth. There were great writers at the other papers—*Melody Maker* had Jon Savage and Richard Williams, *Sounds* had Dave McCullough—but the lion's share was at *NME*. Charged up by its stature as market leader, *NME* saw itself as a

"Charged up by its stature as market leader, *NME* saw itself as a vanguard. Not just a guide for consumers but a cultural arbiter, one whose responsibility was not merely to report what was popular or emerging, but to *decide* what was relevant and progressive."

vanguard. Not just a guide for consumers but a cultural arbiter, one whose responsibility was not merely to report what was popular or emerging, but to *decide* what was relevant and progressive. [2]

What interests me here, though, is not so much the specific ideas, values, assumptions, and biases transmitted by the music papers at that time to moldable young minds like mine, but more the general experience of reading those magazines and how that contrasts with the practice of keeping up with music discourse in an era when it's almost completely mediated by the internet. For if I had happened to have been into Oi! bands like Cockney Rejects, or NWBHM acts like Saxon and Iron Maiden, I would have experienced similar sensations—the clarity of truth hitting you like a smack to the face, the rallying drive of mobilization for the Cause—when reading the frontline dispatches of *Sounds*' Garry Bushell (an accomplished rhetorician and perceptive writer, largely forgotten because he backed horses that have not subsequently galloped their way into history because they didn't get books written about them). There was something structural about the UK music papers that generated particular intensities and energy flows. It had to do with the relation between the readership and the writers, and a particular organization of location and distance, center and periphery. Most of all, it came through the weekly rhythm itself.

If I were to condense all the interrelated aspects of the print-and-paper music press into a handful of words, they'd be synchrony, concentration, relative durability, institutional aura, and authority. All elements that have either been depleted and damaged, or have completely vanished, in the current online music media.

To talk about the systemic virtues of a bygone mode of cultural transmission is to risk scorn. In a culture that idolizes technology and makes secular gods of figures like Steve Jobs and Mark Zuckerberg, it has become inadmissible to talk about change as anything but an a priori positive. And when these changes have taken place within the context of pop music, one also confronts youth's reflexive patriotism for its own era, the way that hormonal triumphalism meshes with generational self-image to insist that only right now can be the best time. I understand that; I've felt that myself. I also know that change is inevitable, irreversible. But I don't see why one shouldn't attempt a calm and clear assessment of what's been lost with the collapse and disappearance of the old ways.

[2] So *NME* simply refused to cover Oi! and the New Wave of British Heavy Metal, apart from the occasional disparaging review, and left these considerable gaps in the market to be exploited by *Sounds*, whose charismatic star writer Garry Bushell championed a series of working class street sounds like the mod revival, 2-Tone, and "Real Punk" aka Oi!

Like any good post-punker and fan of feminist girl-bands like the Slits, Delta 5, and Au Pairs, I was appalled by the resurgent metal's misogyny and machismo, its phallic-ballistic imagery and warrior-male wank fantasies. Reading a particularly eloquent and caustic *NME* review by Paul Du Noyer of a bunch of new metal albums, I was so charged up I took the battle to the streets, transforming chunks of the review into a leaflet that I photocopied and distributed to bemused passersby on the main street of my hometown Berkhamsted. (I was also bored and up for a prank, but the metal disapproval was totally sincere. Nowadays I love AC/DC and can enjoy even the odd Scorpions tune, though I'm not sure if this is progress or decline.)

THE RISE AND FALL OF MALCOLM McLAREN / Part Three

Last Tango in Paris:

'JE NE REGRETTE RIEN...'

MALCOLM McLAREN

SID VICIOUS

by MICHAEL WATTS

WHEN HE WAS LYING, HE WAS MORE INTERESTING THAN MANY MEN TELLING A STORY TRULY.

AN air of unfulfilment and decline hung over 1978. Johnny Rotten, whom Malcolm McLaren had dismissed from the Sex Pistols, had given the band its real sense of style, its fine and murderous edge. Without his malevolent wit, the Pistols' humour was merely brutal. "Belsen Was A Gas" — which Rotten had, in fact, sung in San Francisco but which McLaren insisted on recording again with Ronnie Biggs — was nasty and outrageous but pointless: its anti-semitism didn't threaten any status quo.

The group's focus now became Sid Vicious, previously its sideshow, and in his life the elements of shock and tragedy were rapidly cohering. Paul Cook and Steve Jones, ever the fellow-travellers, still had faith in McLaren, and yet increasingly they were caught up in his recriminations with Rotten and Virgin and alienated by Vicious' difficult behaviour; having some ambition as musicians, they hankered after a less complicated existence of performing and ligging.

McLaren was still obsessed with Rotten; he knew only too well his value to the Pistols. And so Glitterbest monitored all of Rotten's activities. They thought of him as a defector, a Burgess or a Maclean gone over to the enemy — which was the record companies, and specifically Virgin. Their attitude was uncannily like that of the

Situationists, the Sixties' anarchist group with which McLaren and Jamie Reid had sympathised: they, too, had rancorously pursued members who had been expelled or had resigned.

In February, only weeks after the American tour, Rotten returned to Los Angeles with his mother for a holiday and to talk to Warner Bros. The trip was at Warners' expense (he is the only Pistol who still has a firm deal with Warners, although the company has first refusal on all Pistols' material in the States).

He had not long been back in England when he flew out to Jamaica for another holiday and another bit of business with Richard Branson, the head of Virgin Records, and Rudy Van Egmond, a Virgin record-plugger: Branson was using his ear for reggae music in signing acts for Virgin's Front Line reggae label, as well as employing the time to sound out Rotten on his own future. Virgin now found itself in an awkward situation dealing with the two camps of Rotten and Glitterbest.

McLaren, however, put a different interpretation on all this. When two members of Devo, who were then negotiating a contentious signing to Virgin, went out to JA to speak to Branson, McLaren immediately decided that there was a clandestine attempt afoot to make Rotten the American band's lead singer. He later claimed that everyone had been sworn to secrecy: back in England Branson had made Van Egmond sign a piece of paper that he would not divulge the details of the meeting ("I don't think John even met them!" Branson replies with incredulous laughter). A year later, at McLaren's court hearing, Van Egmond made out an affidavit supporting Glitterbest: by then he had left Virgin.

Also out in Jamaica was Boogie (John Tiberi), the Pistols' tour manager and Glitterbest's odd-job man, whom McLaren had dispatched in a spirit of mischief. He was there to obtain film of Rotten being confronted with the immortal line, " Who Killed Bambi? ", but he was actually reduced to filming Rotten from behind bushes as he left hotels and interviewing Tapper Zukie about him.

Boogie says there was another purpose, however: "I was to get him to one side and ask him what he wanted to do." But Rotten remained contemptuously aloof, and Glitterbest set their bearings by his utter rejection of them. McLaren came to believe that Rotten and Branson were in cahoots against him. Virgin and Warner Bros, he said, had whisked Rotten away from him and bust up the Pistols.

His game with the record companies, which had begun when he signed the Pistols to EMI in October 1976, had lost its stirring qualities, had become farcical, but he was working on his moves harder than ever. He used the tapes made with Ronnie Biggs, for example, as a means of testing his limits with Virgin. Should the company not accept Biggs as the new leader of the Pistols, then he would be able, under the terms of the Pistols' agreement, to walk out and negotiate with someone else.

Branson, who also enjoys gamesmanship, responded by trying to sign up the rest of the Great Train Robbers and in anticipation he even had a cake baked in the shape of a train; but they were already contracted to W. H. Allen, who were publishing their story (written by novelist Piers Paul Read).

He eventually accepted the idea of Biggs, but it was a matter of pride to him that he did not capitulate as EMI and A&M had

done. Although he often found McLaren's brazenness amusing, it also alarmed him; he knew he had to be on his toes.

"We had to watch Malcolm," he admits. "There was always the danger that he'd try to rip us off, and he'd have been proud of it. So we were always wary."

However, like other record company figures, Branson recognised that McLaren was not motivated by money alone, and that he had qualities which made him valuable. The music industry chose to think of McLaren as a born publicist and trend-maker, controversial and rather unstable, but gifted with new ideas for marketing acts; it accepted him as a lord of misrule, and up to a point smiled indulgently upon his antics because ultimately it did not believe in all

his wild talk. He was exotic, but there was probably a place for him.

"He's one of a kind," said Bob Regehr at Warner Bros, whose vision of exploding the Pistols upon America was rudely shattered by McLaren's ultimatum to Rotten. "I've never met another manager like him." His tone was suitably chastened.

EVEN after Rotten left the Sex Pistols, McLaren's ideas and personality continued to grip both industry bigwigs and young bands

continued overleaf

"When he was lying, he was more interesting than many men telling a story truly." Published by *Melody Maker* in three installments during June 1979, the tale of Sex Pistols manager Malcolm McLaren served as a requiem for punk and an inquest into recent world-shaking history.

First, a brief history of the British music weeklies. The oldest, *Melody Maker*, started way back in 1926 and covered jazz and dance bands. By the late 1960s it had evolved into the serious rock fan's paper, covering progressive music, which was then known as the Underground. Aimed at teen pop fans, *NME* sold a lot but had little credibility. Then, around 1973, it went through a drastic reinvention by recruiting the sharpest, most irreverent writers from the underground press (those small independent magazines like *IT* and *Oz* founded in the late '60s to cover the British counterculture). This new *New Musical Express* latched onto anything that wasn't a hangover from the longhair '60s, which included movements like glam and pub rock. *NME* rocketed ahead of the now fusty, po-faced *MM*, leaving it to jostle for second place in the circulation wars with *Sounds*, a younger longhair rag oriented more toward hard rock than prog. Nonetheless *Sounds* and *MM* were both slightly ahead of *NME* in supporting punk. *NME*, however, ultimately made punk its own, partly by recruiting some genuine working class writers (a rarity in the graduate-filled, bourgeois-bohemian music press) in the form of Julie Burchill and Tony Parsons, who rapidly became cult figures, then defected to the big league of proper newspapers and glossy mags.

Burchill was the first rock writer whose byline I looked out for. Like so many others, I was hooked by her whiplash wit and by the amphetamine rush she transmitted through the absolute clarity and absolutist confidence of her judgments. "Liberal" was the big punk insult at that time. But unlike every other punk rocker, Burchill (a self-professed communist and Stalin admirer who thought individualism overrated) never lapsed back into easygoing tolerance for different viewpoints, never relented in her bipolar vision. In a famous Singles Review

column from October 1980, Burchill railed against "Rock's Rich Tapestry," her nickname for an ecumenical eclecticism she regarded as weak-minded, and which contrasted with her own belief that the only music that mattered was the Sex Pistols and Motown. Back in those days, a Singles Review could actually become famous if the writer used the format as a launch pad for a manifesto or clarion call. Instead of just directing you to the seven-inches worthy of spending your pocket money on that week, the column could change how people thought about music. It could even influence the mindset of young emerging bands. "Rock's Rich Tapestry" was partial inspiration for Wah! frontman Pete Wylie's formulation of the term "rockism," a concept that is still with us today.

Starting with the Michael Watts piece on McLaren and followed by Burchill articles like her iconoclastic demolition job on James Dean as cult hero (written with co-assassin Parsons, a lapsed Dean fan), I started to cut out and keep particularly thrilling bits of music journalism, gluing them into a scrapbook at first and later keeping them loose in an old battered school briefcase. Soon it was stuffed with features, reviews, and think pieces by Paul Morley, Ian Penman, Barney Hoskyns, and others, the majority snipped from *NME*. (Some music paper fiends kept entire runs of music papers in pristine stacks, but I didn't have the space, something I would regret enormously later). Through rereading these articles over the months and years, there are passages I can recite virtually verbatim, in the same way that poetry fans in previous centuries memorized long stretches of verse.

An *NME* or *Sounds* or *MM* would lie around the house, or your bedroom, for a whole week. You'd pick it up repeatedly during the many yawning longueurs that characterized an era with few distractions. (There was no internet and no video recorders or Tivo; the UK had just three TV channels, largely devoid of interest, and a national pop radio station that only came alive after 6 pm). Most likely you would end up reading the bulk of the issue by the week's end, but you would also find yourself rereading the pieces that had really sparked your imagination. The words and ideas and provocations would lodge in your brain, germinate. Who has time to reread anything these days?

In the pre-digital era, news and views came in concentrated blocks delivered punctually at regular intervals, rather than the constant drip feed, omnidirectional info blitz that we have today. A weekly or monthly music magazine was bundled and definitive, unchangeable once printed onto paper and inseparable once stapled/folded/glued together. Like me you could cut out pieces or pull out pages, but that required more effort and intent than today's idle bookmarking and pasting-and-saving. For most people any given issue remained intact, a distinct entity unto itself.

Bundling meant that each issue served as a cross section of what was going on in that week or month as determined by the editorial perspective and filtering decisions of each magazine. If that issue was then kept, it provided a snapshot of its era, a zeitgeist slice that would live indefinitely. Bundling also created the feeling of a world, a climate of sensibility and shared values. This came through not just the editorial choices and the range of writing styles and viewpoints on offer, but via the myriad small yet crucial decisions pertaining to typography, layout, photographs, and illustrations, as well as the various opportunities for collective voice and "vibe" presented by the readers' letters page (with its replies from a staff member or contributor given the chore that week), the picture captions and headlines, the gossip column, and so on. Subliminal to a reader at the time but still part of the magazine's texture (and valuable data for today's historians) were the non-editorial components like the adverts for records and tours (along with youth-oriented products of all kinds), the back page musicians ads, and the more functional service-oriented sections like news and gig listings.

What the music papers I grew up on offered was a concentrated, all-enveloping experience that allowed you to escape from your real surroundings, with all their dreary limitations, and achieve vicarious access to the place where all the action was happening and all the ideas were percolating. Concentration of a different kind was involved in reading the frequently very long features. It's

> "What the music papers I grew up on offered was a concentrated, all-enveloping experience that allowed you to escape from your real surroundings, with all their dreary limitations, and achieve vicarious access to the place where all the action was happening and all the ideas were percolating."

perfectly possible, of course, to flick desultorily through a printed magazine in just the same way one drifts shiftlessly across the infosphere. But something about the bound nature of the magazine encourages getting pulled into a story, and staying with it until the end.

Few online magazines have been able to create this effect of enclosure and focus. On the internet, newspapers and magazines are permeable and the reader's attention is too often fatally distracted by the adjacencies of any given webpage to…everything else in the online universe. Hyperlinks, those editorially self-inflicted wounds, encourage interruptions to the reading process, diversions that may never return to the main road. Some webzines sabotage their own writers by attempting to increase

overall clicks, tantalizing the reader's attention with a constant flicker of options for further reading within the site. Aggregation (para)sites attack the tenuous integrity of online magazines, literally breaking them to pieces, undermining their vain vestigial efforts to establish a coherent editorial vision and institutional vibe.

I've been using "concentration" to refer both to the density and volume of music writing gathered in a single place, and the sustained attention it provoked and demanded. But there's another facet to concentration relevant here: the accumulation of power and influence, and the weight this gave to a magazine's opinions.

Because there were three main papers (*Record Mirror* was really a kid brother, closer to the *NME* back when it had been a teen-oriented rag), this meant that any album or single received just three verdicts that counted. Other opinions existed but you really had to search them out. [3]

⇒══════⇐

In their heyday—approximately 1968 to 1983—the UK weekly music papers had the field almost to themselves. The regularity of publication, the copiousness and penetration of the coverage, the blend of professional magazine polish with passion, polemic and pretentiousness levels closer to the fiery fanzines—all of this made the inkies the only "place" to be, whether as a reader or as an aspiring writer. These were the opinions that mattered, and for most people, the only opinions one encountered. In the UK at that time, it was very hard to access American rock writing. *Rolling Stone* was available but I never knew anyone who read it, and it seemed to largely cover artists that were Old Wave, at least according to the British perspective. I never once saw *Creem* and I'm fairly sure I didn't even know it existed. I only discovered that *The Village Voice* was a

bastion of intellectually serious rock writing on my first journalistic trip to New York in 1987. Now and then I tried to find it in London but it was only available, seemingly, in Tower Records, as a prohibitively expensive import.

Nowadays there are vastly more outlets for opinion and information about music, and one can access the majority of what's written in the English language from anywhere in the world, in most cases free of cost. I have severe doubts whether this is a net positive, though; certainly, there's a case for "less is more." When a major release rolls out—a *Random Access Memories*, a *Modern Vampires of the City*—virtually every available position on the spectrum of potential opinion is taken up by someone. This superabundance and redundancy of opinion has deleterious effects on both readers and writers.

For the writers, it can feel like adding one's voice to the hubbub is pointless. In the more reduced media environment of the weekly music press, I get the sense that the writers raised their game because they knew that when they weighed in, their judgments had weight; there was power but also responsibility. Heterodox opinions seemed to have more impact too: Ian Penman heading the opposite direction to the critical herd with his skeptical take on PiL's *Flowers of Romance*, Barney Hoskyns's abstention from the ABC hype and dissident enthusiasm for the sickness and self-destruction of The Birthday Party. For today's readers, numbed exhaustion is the all too likely upshot of an accelerated media ecology where the forelash, the backlash, the backlash against the backlash, and the studiously reasonable and fair-minded in-between view, follow in lightning quick succession, often before one has had a chance to hear the record. With event releases, every possible permutation of commentary, including commentary about the commentary, is wrung out in pursuit of incremental bumps in traffic. The predicament is not unique to music, of course—you

---

[3] There was *ZigZag*, an independently owned monthly originally oriented to the Underground, with a particular bias towards West Coast rock, but then gradually evolving through punk and post-punk to become a goth-focused publication. During the early-to-mid '70s there'd been *Let It Rock*, *Streetlife*, and *Cream* (no relation to *Creem* in the U.S.) but they too had never sold much and were gone by the time I started reading. You could sometimes find incisive coverage of youth culture in left-wing publications like *New Statesman* and *New Society*. There were a few intelligent voices in the quality national newspapers, or in London's listings magazine *Time Out*. But pop coverage in "proper" mags tended to be restrained and well-behaved, with none of the inflammatory power of the inkies at their most unleashed and stylistically adventurous. By the early 1980s, you had also the "style bibles". *The Face*, initially barely more than a monthly *NME* with better photography, gradually developed a distinct character based on its uneasy mix of clubland and fashion trendspotting with edgy current affairs features, the mélange unified by a stark design aesthetic. *iD* started as a striking-looking, pictorially dominated zine documenting cutting-edge street fashion but, like *The Face*, gradually incorporated some excellent popcult writing. Both "stylies" would eventually eclipse the inkies, making them look old fashioned, but this really only took off in the mid-to-late 1980s.

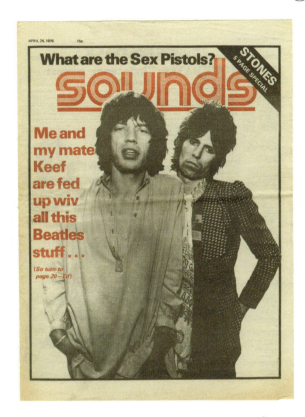

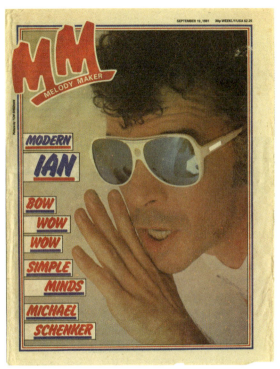

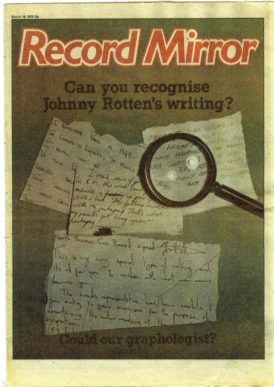

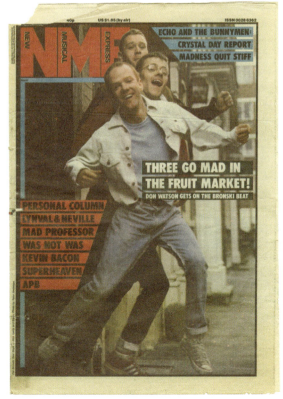

get the same kind of real-time forensic analysis in political news (which covers not only events, but also the "optics" of events, building layers of speculation upon conjecture upon speculation), and in dramatic television, with the hyper-exegesis applied to series like *Mad Men*.

One side effect of saturation coverage is that you find yourself reading faster to keep up with it all, skimming through the texts, which then leave a fainter imprint on your memory. Again, the weekly rhythms of the old music press allowed for a more manageable tempo of ingestion and digestion. When I first started spending large chunks of time in America, back in the early 1990s, I noticed that there was a time gulf between the UK and the U.S. The cultural metabolism of the music scene felt much slower in the States, where magazines were monthly and singles took a while to gather radio momentum and scale the charts. These days, thanks to the internet, America and the UK are totally synchronized, both subject to the remorseless schedule of the hourly news cycle and the instant update. The pace of the weekly music press I grew up with, and later contributed to, now seems almost indolent by comparison. Yet in contrasting then and now, I find the weekly cycle to be just about perfect: fast enough to fuel a feeling of cultural acceleration, slow enough that you could fully absorb what you were reading and hearing.

As a reader in the late 1970s and early 1980s, and as a writer (for *Melody Maker*) in the late 1980s and early 1990s, I recall the way that any striking stance or provocative idea would trigger both complementary and opposing views in the next issue. Allies took the baton and ran further with it, while rivals and enemies took violent exception. That still happens on the internet, with Tumblrs and tweets, but in a much more accelerated and ephemeral way. A week feels to me like the ideal interval for the formulation of a considered response.

With its superfluity of options, its decentralized focus, and the blurring of past and present into what William Gibson calls "atemporality," the internet stokes a restless, distracted, omnivorous music libido, the opposite of the intense and lasting attachment fans gave to a single generation-defining band like Joy Division or Nirvana, or to a movement like punk or rave.

I'm using words like libido and desire, but what I'm really talking about is a certain lovelessness that has crept into music fandom and music writing. Love is the relation one has to another person where you are not just looking for specific satisfactions (sex, companionship,

support, etc.), but seeking the Answer to the existential question that is you. True love is born out of lack, a sense of incompleteness. It is a religion of one, a utopian belief system with an attainable, if idealized, object. The parallels between this and music love aren't watertight: very few people are dedicated only to one artist, and not many people listen exclusively to just one genre. Nonetheless, there is something to the idea that an environment of saturating plenitude, where there are always many other fish in the sea and hooking up is near instantaneous and effortless, is not conducive to true musical passion. It's been said that today we like a lot but love little. Pleasure-attuned agnosticism becomes the norm. We nibble eclectically at Pop's Rich Tapas Bar.

In romantic love and in music fandom, absences and delays create the space in which desire grows. The remoteness in space or time of the "unattainable" or "yet to come" fills the present with exquisite tension, a forward-directed propulsion. In an "always on," instant access world, the flooding nowness and nearness of everything unavoidably smothers and stifles these impulses. It kills not just yearning, but eventually appetite too.

In *A Lover's Discourse*, Roland Barthes defines the lover as "precisely... the one who waits." Lou Reed's version of the same idea (albeit based around a romance with a chemical not a person) is "first thing you learn is that you always gotta wait." Addiction, obsession, love: the appeal of these painful, pang-full states of being may have to do in part with the way they manage time, structuring one's life around the principles of rarity and intermittence. But where Barthes and Reed are both talking about a relationship of power—being under another's control, experiencing an anxiety of abandonment that can escalate into delirium—there's also a more positive aspect to the deferment and suspension. Waiting heightens the intensity, the weight of an event when it finally occurs. In the words of Delta 5—a band I would have read about in *NME* some Wednesday or other, or might have heard on John Peel's BBC radio show had I waited until 10 pm and sat patiently through the program itself—"anticipation is so much better." ✏

Simon Reynolds wrote for Melody Maker *from 1986 to 1996. He is the author of seven books including the post-punk history* Rip It Up and Start Again, *the rave chronicle* Energy Flash, *and* Retromania. *Born in London and a resident of New York for many years, he now lives in Los Angeles.*

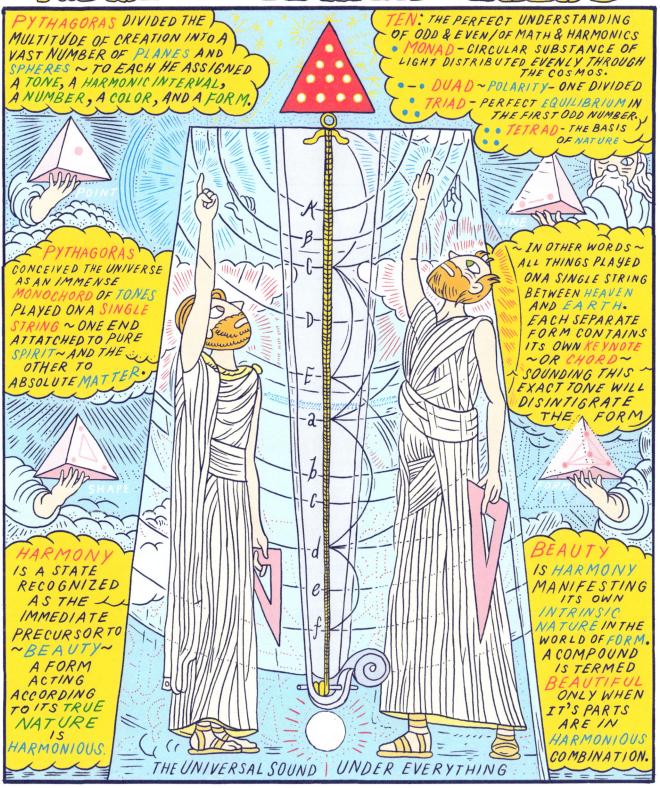

THE MUNDANE MONOCHORD

PYTHAGORAS DIVIDED THE MULTITUDE OF CREATION INTO A VAST NUMBER OF PLANES AND SPHERES ~ TO EACH HE ASSIGNED A TONE, A HARMONIC INTERVAL, A NUMBER, A COLOR, AND A FORM.

TEN: THE PERFECT UNDERSTANDING OF ODD & EVEN / OF MATH & HARMONICS
• **MONAD** - CIRCULAR SUBSTANCE OF LIGHT DISTRIBUTED EVENLY THROUGH THE COSMOS.
•--• **DUAD** ~ POLARITY - ONE DIVIDED
TRIAD - PERFECT EQUILIBRIUM IN THE FIRST ODD NUMBER.
TETRAD - THE BASIS OF NATURE

PYTHAGORAS CONCEIVED THE UNIVERSE AS AN IMMENSE MONOCHORD OF TONES PLAYED ON A SINGLE STRING ~ ONE END ATTACHED TO PURE SPIRIT ~ AND THE OTHER TO ABSOLUTE MATTER.

~ IN OTHER WORDS ~ ALL THINGS PLAYED ON A SINGLE STRING BETWEEN HEAVEN AND EARTH. EACH SEPARATE FORM CONTAINS ITS OWN KEYNOTE ~ OR CHORD ~ SOUNDING THIS EXACT TONE WILL DISINTIGRATE THE FORM

POINT

LINE

SHAPE

FORM

A B C D E a b c d e f

HARMONY IS A STATE RECOGNIZED AS THE IMMEDIATE PRECURSOR TO ~ BEAUTY ~ A FORM ACTING ACCORDING TO ITS TRUE NATURE IS HARMONIOUS.

BEAUTY IS HARMONY MANIFESTING ITS OWN INTRINSIC NATURE IN THE WORLD OF FORM. A COMPOUND IS TERMED BEAUTIFUL ONLY WHEN IT'S PARTS ARE IN HARMONIOUS COMBINATION.

THE UNIVERSAL SOUND | UNDER EVERYTHING

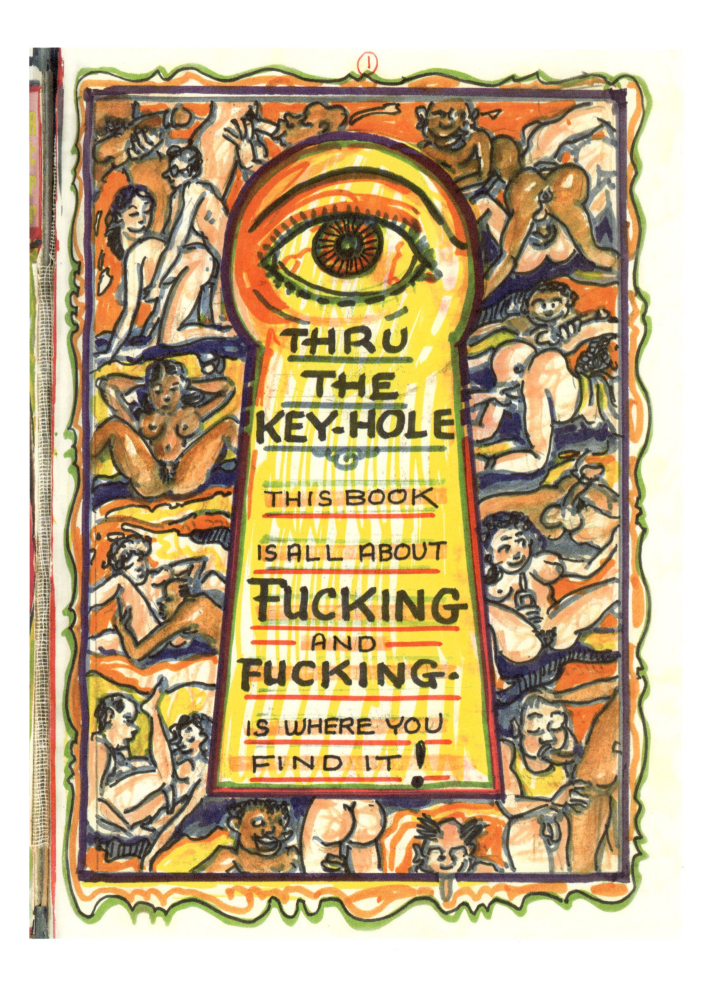

Fucking Is Where You Find It!

The drawing board antics of
fiddle and mandolin player
Howard "Louie Bluie" Armstrong.

BY AMANDA PETRUSICH

I saw Howard Armstrong's work before I heard it. It was a counterintuitive introduction to a fiddle player, maybe, but not for one whose extant 78 rpm records each hover in the one to three known copies range, and whose glowing, hand-drawn illustrations carry titles like "Titties!" and "My Dick".

I was visiting the collector and record producer Christopher King at his home in Faber, Virginia, about 30 miles southwest of Charlottesville. King is a sought-after, Grammy-winning audio engineer with a particular knack for massaging usable sound from scraped-up, gouged-out 78s, and what I was really after in Virginia was a chance to hear his copy of Blind Uncle Gaspard's "Sur Le Borde de L'Eau", a Cajun ballad recorded for Vocalion Records in February of 1929. It is a breathtaking performance: Gaspard's voice is so saturated with longing that it seems to hover midair, like a helium balloon that has lost too much gas. It is tenuous and beautiful and then it disintegrates entirely. King had just acquired a copy via some mysterious, multifaceted negotiation with a man whose name he was reluctant to reveal. I was working on a book about rare 78 rpm records and the men who kept them; these sorts of high-stakes, high-intrigue transactions had come to occupy a disproportionate amount of my attention.

King ushered me into his studio and handed me a glass of Turkish iced tea. By now, we had a pretty good routine going: he would play me rare records and we would talk about the complex practice of collecting or, more often, the mystery of recorded sound and our shared psychic reliance upon it. That was a curiosity we indulged together: how music worked on people, how it worked on us.

Eventually, after a few spins of the Gaspard, King shuffled off and started unwrapping what looked like a large, hand-illustrated Bible. I should say now that King's music room (a dark, cooled spot in a corner of the converted farmhouse he shares with his wife and daughter) contains innumerable delights for fans of archaic or outmoded technologies: antique tube amplifiers, test pressings, prehistoric songbooks. It isn't unusual for remarkable objects to emerge unbidden. One time, when I was gathering my things to leave, he stood up and handed me a tiny brass sheep's bell from Albania, where he had just spent some time field-recording indigenous Epirotic laments. These are the sort of things he fetches from his drawers.

A few weeks earlier, I'd had plans to accompany King on a fact-finding trip to the Blue Ridge Music Center in

"It is an art-store sketchbook crammed with marker illustrations and collages of people engaged in various lewd activities, one for each letter of the alphabet."

nearby Galax, but Hurricane Sandy had kept me marooned in New York City, drinking ungodly amounts of rye whiskey and, like everyone else in town, chewing my fingernails to nubs. I knew he'd acquired something noteworthy and unexpected on that trip, but I didn't know precisely what it was (King has a penchant for the dramatic, well-timed reveal). He tugged off the last bit of tissue paper and handed me the book. I opened it to a picture of a woman doing herself with a white dildo. At the top, someone had written "Bed Room Antics". I turned it over to look at the cover, which featured a large African-American woman masturbating, the tip of one nipple ensconced in her mouth, and the words, "Fucking Is Where You Find It!"

(The "Is Where You Find It!" part was written inside a little ink drawing of an erect penis.)

The book was drawn (or assembled—some images, like the woman of "Bed Room Antics", were clipped from specialty periodicals) by the fiddle and mandolin player Howard Armstrong between 1989 and 1990. This was several decades after Armstrong's initial run as a member of the Tennessee Chocolate Drops, the string band he started with his brother, Roland Armstrong, and the Piedmont blues vocalist and guitarist Carl Martin in 1930 (nearly 80 years later, their name would inspire the Carolina Chocolate Drops, another black string band). He recorded a handful of 78 rpm records in the late 1920s and early 1930s as the Tennessee Chocolate Drops or with Ted

28

Bogan as Louie Bluie—the nom-de-plume he adopted in 1932 after a woman mistook him for Louis Armstrong. These are now highly coveted slabs of shellac, in part because they are terrifically rare, but mostly because Armstrong is a generous, gleeful player, a showman in the style of Uncle Dave Macon or Memphis Minnie, but with a savant-like ease on his instruments.

Armstrong's musical legacy is significant in that it represents an under-mythologized facet of pre-war vernacular music—namely, black musicians playing the string band music more typically associated with Appalachian whites. "Armstrong is playing what is essentially a pre-blues, hillbilly repertoire. That same music was being played in white and black communities," King said of Armstrong's records. "That's his importance—he represents this very lost tradition of black string band performers. There were very few that survived. In the first part of the 20th century, an awful lot of the best performers of hillbilly music were not hillbillies."

In 1979, the filmmaker Terry Zwigoff—who would later produce and direct the documentary

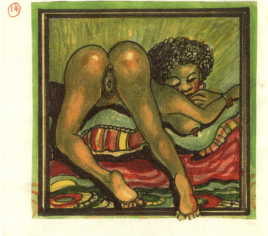

Crumb and the feature *Ghost World*, two of the finest cinematic expressions of the mania of 78 collecting—became obsessed with Armstrong's rendition of "State Street Rag",v a quick-footed, rollicking guitar-and-mandolin tune Armstrong wrote and recorded with Bogan on March 23, 1934, in Chicago, in a session for Bluebird Records. There are less than five known copies of that particular 78 left, and, as is often the case with pre-war vernacular music, no metal masters of the recording. It's a spectacular performance—undeniable and immediate, like a child zooming across the room for a hug. Zwigoff hunted Armstrong down, and spent the subsequent six

years filming him for an hour-long documentary, *Louie Bluie*, which was finally reissued by Criterion in 2010 (Zwigoff has said the film stock was already beginning to decompose when Criterion intervened).

By the 1970s, Armstrong had relocated to Detroit (he was born and reared in Tennessee) to take a job in the auto industry. The folk revival of the late 1960s—the same search-and-rescue that resurrected the careers of Delta bluesmen like Son House, Skip James, and Mississippi John Hurt—had allowed him to start playing around a bit for cash. People were interested in the old songs again.

There are many unexpectedly captivating scenes in *Louie Bluie*—like when Armstrong makes himself a serving of Hills Bros. instant coffee by boiling water in a cast iron frying pan and carefully pouring it into a teacup, or when he and Bogan play a raucous version of "State Street Rag" for an unmoved Yank Rachell who is relaxing nearby, reading the Pennysaver and occasionally peering over his eyeglasses. Arguably the most enthralling is when Armstrong sits down in an art gallery with his buddy Ike.

The relationship is not explained. Armstrong wears a beret. He carefully, ceremoniously unlocks a small briefcase and pulls out what he calls a "Whorehouse Bible", or *The ABCs of Pornography*. It is an art store sketchbook crammed with marker illustrations and collages of people engaged in various lewd activities, one for each letter of the alphabet. Armstrong hands it to Ike, who is in a jacket and tie, and giggling nervously. He makes sounds while he flips the pages, "Hoo-eee!"

"I think there's a little knowledge that can be gained if you read the book all the way through, about different

SIGNS OF WISDOM THAT WE HATE TO READ.

TRY ME BEFORE YOU TRY THEM— I PROMISE TO LEAVE YOU MORE TO PUT IN THE GROUND WHEN I AM THRU WITH YOU.—DR. NUTTALL MD.

WHEN YOU'RE DEALING WITH THE WRONG PUSSY, BE SURE YOU HAVE THE RIGHT INSURANCE
LAY-A-WAY BURIAL SOCIETY
PAY NOW — GO LATER

DON'T GET CARRIED AWAY WHILE YOU'RE ENJOYING SOME STOLEN PUSSY — WE'LL DO IT FOR YOU WHEN YOU GET CAUGHT
READY-TO-ROLL AMBULANCE SERVICE —

APARTHEID
RACISM IN SOUTH AFRICA

THERE'S AN UGLINESS IN SOUTH AFRICA
THEY CALL IT — "APARTHEID" —
IT'S AN EVIL THING — TO INTER-
RACIAL SWING — THE RACISTS SPREAD
IT FAR AND WIDE —
THEY SAY: "WHITE IS RIGHT- KEEP
WHITE ON WHITE!" SO THE FORCES
OF HATE STILL PUSH — TO GIVE THE WHITE
MAN- THE RULING HAND AND KEEP THE
BLACK MAN IN THE BUSH.—
THINGS DON'T ALWAYS WORK OUT AS THEY
PLAN THEM — THIS, I AM HAPPY TO SAY,
THE BLACK "KAFFIR" GETS IN MEM-
SAHIB'S "FUR" WHEN THE WHITE BAAS IS
AWAY!

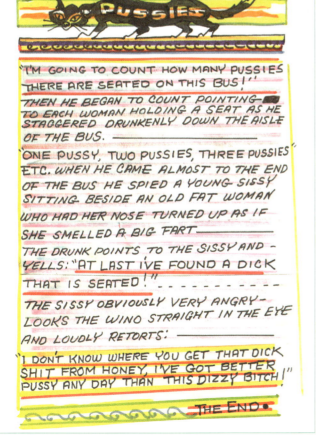

PUSSIES

"I'M GOING TO COUNT HOW MANY PUSSIES THERE ARE SEATED ON THIS BUS!"
THEN HE BEGAN TO COUNT POINTING TO EACH WOMAN HOLDING A SEAT AS HE STAGGERED DRUNKENLY DOWN THE AISLE OF THE BUS. —
ONE PUSSY, TWO PUSSIES, THREE PUSSIES ETC. WHEN HE CAME ALMOST TO THE END OF THE BUS HE SPIED A YOUNG SISSY SITTING BESIDE AN OLD FAT WOMAN WHO HAD HER NOSE TURNED UP AS IF SHE SMELLED A BIG FART—
THE DRUNK POINTS TO THE SISSY AND - YELLS:"AT LAST I'VE FOUND A DICK THAT IS SEATED!" - - - - - - -
THE SISSY OBVIOUSLY VERY ANGRY- LOOKS THE WINO STRAIGHT IN THE EYE AND LOUDLY RETORTS: —
"I DON'T KNOW WHERE YOU GET THAT DICK SHIT FROM HONEY, I'VE GOT BETTER PUSSY ANY DAY THAN THIS DIZZY BITCH!"

THE END.

PUSSIES

AN OLD DRUNK BOARDED A CITY BUS AND TO HIS CHAGRIN HE FOUND THAT ALL THE SEATS WERE TAKEN — MOSTLY BY WOMEN...OLD WOMEN, YOUNG WOMEN, — JUST WOMEN.
WITH A BELLY FULL OF WHISKEY WHICH SEEMED TO GROW HEAVIER AND HEAVIER AS THE BUS RODE ON.... SO HE BEGAN TO VERBALIZE HIS DISPLEASURE.
TIMES ARE GOING FROM BAD TO WORSE" HE- RANTED — "A MAN CAN'T GET A SEAT ANYMORE BECAUSE ALL THE CUNTS HAVE TAKEN THEM!"

— CONTINUED →

"He was one of those people who is a storehouse of folklore, stories, jokes, songs, history. He was also a consummate showman."

—ROBERT CRUMB

things that we don't ordinarily hear about," Armstrong says to him. "A lot of people think pornography is something vicious or ugly, but it's a basic part of our lives, believe it or not." Armstrong starts narrating a scene in which a man named Jody—this is the "J" entry—is cooking chitlins in a saucepan, nude from the waist down, while a woman lays open-legged on the bed. Her whole name and address is showing; she's gamely peering up at him, her arms folded behind her head. In the right corner of the page, another man, whom Armstrong identifies as her husband, is slowly opening the front door, lunchbox in hand. "Of course you know what happened, don't you?" Armstrong says.

"This is some book," Ike says.

"Well, sure it's some book. It's special. Make a weak-minded fool go stone crazy."

There is considerable conjecture tossed about by collectors regarding how many of these books exist, and who, since Armstrong's death in 2003 at age 94, has managed to get their hands on them. King wasn't sure of the details. "My understanding is that there are three pornographic bibles, this being one of them," King said, gesturing to *Fucking Is Where You Find It!* "The first one, *The ABCs of Pornography*, was stolen—got swallowed up by a black hole. And it's a hard thing to move. It's like the Pink Panther diamond. How are you gonna move the Pink Panther diamond? How are you gonna move *The ABCs of Pornography*? The third one, I believe, was commissioned and is owned by Terry [Zwigoff] himself."

Armstrong, obviously, was something of a polymath. In the opening moments of *Louie Bluie*, he explains himself, "Sometimes I feel like I'm three or four different people—I want to paint awhile, it'll burn within me, just to paint, paint, paint! Then that cools off, and I want to play my music. Then that'll cool off, and I want to write poetry, I want to do this, I want to do something else. I feel sometimes like Dr. Jekyll and Mr. Hyde."

King, at least, saw something pure and dynamic in the book. "It has a big attraction to me because it's Howard Armstrong, and it does have musical content, although the vast majority is pornographic and dirty and sordid," he explained. "But I think it shows every aspect he's known for—his musicianship, his artistry, his writing, his poetry. It's very honest."

Although these kinds of transactions are often heated, King's acquisition of the book—from the folklorist Joe Wilson, who briefly served as Armstrong's tour manager in the late 1980s— wasn't particularly fraught. "I'd been working with Joe, a man I've known for 20 years, on a variety of projects promoting folk music in the Virginias. He knew I was a big fan of Armstrong," King recounted. "We were talking one day, and he said, 'I know you really like Howard Armstrong. How would you like to have one of his dirty books?' And I said, 'I would really, really like to have one of his dirty books.' So I arranged to go down and visit him [in Galax]. We met at his house, and his wife made some lunch for us, and we went down to the basement, which is where dirty things are supposed to be kept. He took it out, and I started thumbing through it. He didn't know how to value it.

"OH YE DAUGHTERS OF ZION—I AM BLACK BUT I AM COMELY."—FROM THE QUEEN OF SHEBA

He said, 'This is how much I gave Armstrong in cash when he needed cash and we were touring together. At the end of the tour, he said, 'How about I just trade you this book rather than pay you back the cash?' and I agreed." Years later, Wilson agreed to trade it to King for his help with a musical preservation project.

Not all of Armstrong's artwork is pornographic. He's done album covers and portraits, little clusters of broad, grinning faces. He even collaborated with his wife, Barbara, on a children's book based on her Massachusetts childhood. Much of *Fucking Is Where You Find It!* is focused, in one way or another, on the satiation of female desire—the pull of it. There are a lot of women drawn or configured waiting, breathless and longing, for their men. You can almost feel the trembling. Armstrong seemed to take a particular glee in that: satisfying someone. All of the drawn characters are anatomically exaggerated; penises are endless and waving, buttocks are protrusive, round.

There's also plenty of text, little stories and poems conveying various indecent fantasies, inscribed in different colors and fonts. Some, like "My Dick" ("My dick is a powerful thing/ My dick can really swing/ My dick is so big and hard/ The pimps and hustlers keep it barred/ They know they must be on guard from/ My dick"), were forged in earnest homage. But they range in palatability. I'll say only that while they were not endorsed, exactly, pedophilia and bestiality were not off-limits.

Everything is rendered in florescent color, which gives the book a kind of heated exuberance, as if sex weren't already some definition of euphoria. His lines are wobbly, almost animated. The pictures practically move.

Like Robert Crumb's illustrations, Armstrong's draw-

ings are heavily influenced by late 19th-century cartoons. Incidentally, Crumb, who also collects rare 78s, is an ardent fan of Armstrong's musical and artistic output. "I don't have any of Howard Armstrong's 78s," Crumb told me. "They are, unfortunately, extremely rare. I do have one of his oil paintings, however, and one watercolor. I bought them from Howard through the auspices of Terry Zwigoff. I met him a couple of times while Terry was making the film. He was a diamond in the rough. An artistic genius from the bottom level of American society, an uneducated person who was living in a project in the ghetto of Detroit when Terry approached him to make the documentary. He was one of those people who is a storehouse of folklore, stories, jokes, songs, history. He was also a consummate showman. Terry told me that once the camera was rolling, Armstrong was on. The film practically made itself. Terry got lucky when he crossed paths with that man."

Armstrong's raconteurship is foregrounded in *Louie Bluie,* and—insomuch as the question of why he might have made these books is even worth asking; insomuch as titillation is not merely an end in itself—it is obvious that he liked to get people's attention. He liked eyes on him. There is something winking about *Fucking Is Where You Find It!,* and especially in the way Armstrong shows it off to Ike. He is goading us to get a little agitated about it, to linger too long on one image or another. It is a quality I recognize in his records, too: a playfulness, an acquiescence to whatever feels good. There is not a lot of room in his performances for acrimony or staidness.

I asked King what he thought Armstrong got out of it—why he made the books. "I think it was a release," he said. "Just like with anything else, Amanda."

King's notion—that it was a kind of proxy loosening, an external way of channeling, mediating want—made sense. I mean, there's certainly extensive precedent for that sort of thing. King believes we all require a pressure valve of one sort or another, a way to discharge and excise our shitty, counterproductive thoughts. "I think there are a lot of people who do really bad, evil things, shooting up schoolyards, offing themselves, offing others—and I think it's because they don't have another way to express themselves, through music or through writing or through art," he said. "It baffles me sometimes, to think about how every human being has a huge amount of creative potential, but they don't have an avenue for expressing it, they don't have the facilities to do that. People have given up on trying to express themselves, and are just punching keys."

It's an odd exercise, reconciling Armstrong's parallel interests: the gleeful, exuberant fiddling, the parade of prepared genitalia. The build-up and the release. But there is beauty in the way Armstrong conjured and contained his desires.

In whatever it did for him. In whatever it does for us. ✐

Amanda Petrusich is the author of It Still Moves: Lost Songs, Lost Highways, and the Search for the Next American Music *and* Pink Moon. *She is a contributing editor to the* Oxford American *and a contributing writer at* Pitchfork, *and her music and culture writing have appeared in* The New York Times, Spin, The Atlantic, *and elsewhere. Her new book about 78rpm record collectors,* Do Not Sell At Any Price, *is forthcoming from Scribner in 2014. She lives in Brooklyn and teaches writing at NYU.*

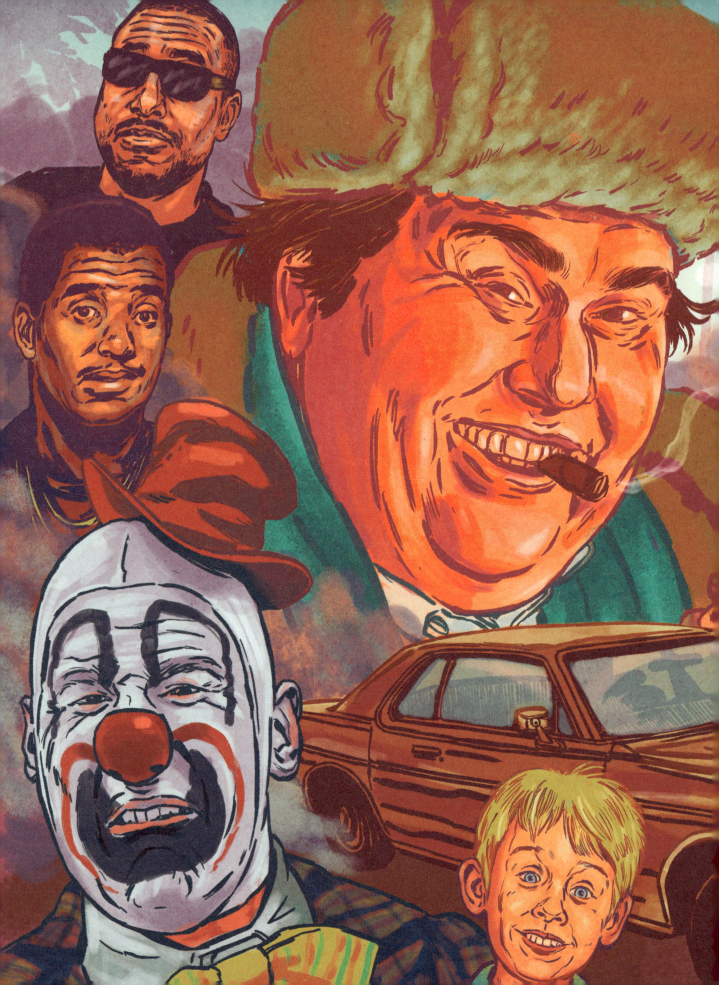

Posse In Effect

The John Hughes-Delicious Vinyl Connection

How the most popular director of the 1980s
and LA's first breakthrough hip-hop label
teamed up to create a John Candy classic.

BY PETER RELIC

ILLUSTRATIONS BY BRANDON LOVING

It was a cool night in January 1989 along a sketchy stretch of Santa Monica Boulevard on an unreconstructed block of central Hollywood. Motion picture director John Hughes and his 13-year-old son stood on the sidewalk before a paint-blistered door beside a shuttered carburetor repair shop. The director—known for his generation-defining blockbusters *The Breakfast Club*, *Pretty In Pink*, and *Ferris Bueller's Day Off*—rapped his knuckles on the door repeatedly to no avail. A "lady" of the night, working the block, smiled and waved at them before stepping into a sedan that pulled up at the curb.

"I'm not sure it was a good idea to bring you here," John Hughes told his son.

"Knock one more time, dad," said John Hughes III.

In the apartment upstairs, a motley crew was watching a VHS dub of *Shaft* and drinking beer. There was 28-year-old Matt Dike, a tall, lank-haired Jehovah's Witness reborn as an underground DJ; Michael Ross, 27, a Long Beach-bred UCLA grad and funk fanatic in a purple Lakers cap; Stephen "Haggis" Harris, ex-bassist for The Cult and founder of hesh-boogie band The Four Horsemen; and Mario Caldato, Jr., a former aircraft machinist from nearby Torrance turned mobile sound system operator.

Almost 25 years later, the details of that night remain vivid in the mind of John Hughes III: "It was 10 or 11 o'clock, and even though no one came to the door, we could hear beats playing upstairs. It was probably five minutes of knocking before someone answered. And then we walked up the stairs and we were in Matt's place." At first glance, the second story railroad flat overstuffed with record LPs and haphazardly-stacked recording equipment didn't look like the natural birthplace of million-selling rap records. Yet Dike's apartment doubled as the creative headquarters of Delicious Vinyl, the upstart record label Dike and Ross had formed less than 18 months earlier. Their marquee rapper—a semi-reformed, gravel-gullet gangster called Tone Lōc—had upset the pop Top 40 with his irrepressible hit "Wild Thing", at the time the second fastest selling single ever behind only "We Are The World". The crossover smash—as well as its follow-up, "Funky Cold Medina"—turned Dike and his creative partner Ross into a production pair possessing a platinum touch in a style of music just awakening to its commercial potential. The territorial significance of the Tone Lōc records was immense too, expanding rap's geographical map all the way to LA, at a time when the culture was still seen as a strictly New York City phenomena.

A work by a renowned Big Apple artist greeted father and son at the top of Dike's stairs that night. "There was a huge door—the size of a wall—that Basquiat had painted," says John Hughes III. (The untitled painting, which remains in Matt Dike's collection to this day, is a radical self-portrait of a twig-limbed, gap-toothed, blank-eyed figure.) "I thought it was just a strange painting, but my father recognized it as a Basquiat. And there was another Basquiat painting just leaning up against the wall. The paintings were not protected and everyone was smoking around them. My dad was like, *Whoa!* It blew my father's mind that it all seemed so casual, but that it was focused and creative."

Before co-founding Delicious Vinyl, Matt Dike worked at Larry Gagosian's LA gallery as Jean-Michel Basquiat's West Coast personal assistant, and Jean-Michel often crashed at Dike's pad when he was in town. Dike's apartment was, in effect, a locus for grimy bohemia. As Delicious Vinyl's in-house sound engineer Mario Caldato, Jr. explains: "It wasn't like, 'Oh, some big director is coming over!' People were always showing up at Dike's pad—musicians and producers and actors and friends from nightclubs. There was pretty much an open-door policy, but we were getting work done, too. So on any given night you might have John Lurie crashing on the couch, or Malcolm McLaren hanging out, but no one got special treatment."

This latter fact must have appealed to the executive-averse John Hughes. His son John explains: "Our family had lived in LA from 1984 to 1988, then we moved to Chicago, because my dad didn't really want us being brought up in Hollywood and all that goes with that. I was around so many people in my dad's business who did the total kiss-ass version of meeting John Hughes' son. Mike [Ross] and Matt [Dike] were not like that. When

I found out my dad was going to meet Matt and Mike, I begged him to take me with him. I'd been doing music on a boom box with a dual tape deck and a four-track when that was all I had for gear, and my dad saw I was super interested in that. He bought a Roland Juno 60 synthesizer and E-mu Drumulator and would play around on them, and leave them around for me to play with. My dad pulled me out of school so many times...this was one of those times."

The purpose of John Hughes' visit was to see if Dike and Ross would agree to Tone Lōc's "Wild Thing" being used in a scene from his upcoming movie, the John Candy-commanded comedy *Uncle Buck*. During an early test screening of the film, Tone's jam played as temp music in a scene where Candy's Buck character dances down a high school hallway after a tendentious tête-à-tête with a wart-faced principal. "Apparently the audience went completely nuts when 'Wild Thing' started," says Matt Dike, "and Hughes was sitting there at the screening watching people lose their shit and was like, 'Oh, we've got to use that song. I've got to meet those guys.'"

Hughes' arrival at Dike's place was driven in part by core curiosity—before becoming a director, he worked in the 1970s as a writer at anti-establishment humor magazine *National Lampoon*, where he learned facets of the craft from *Lampoon* superstar Doug Kenney (who would script both *Animal House* and *Caddyshack*). Much as the *Lampoon*'s editorial offices had functioned as a manic hothouse of creativity and misbehavior, so did Dike's apartment double as a place where just about anyone was welcome to drop in at anytime to hang out and, perhaps, contribute ideas to the music.

In the zone, slightly stoned, Matt Dike and Michael Ross were listening to a fresh batch of beats they had cooked up, as well as playing back an early mix of a song by a hyper-verbose super-nerd named Young MC called "Make That Move" (later renamed "Bust A Move"). It was a typical funky night at Matt's. And as soon as he heard the different beats they were playing, Hughes knew that this was the music that would complete his new movie.

B uck Russell is rooting around in his precariously packed closet. His brother and his brother's wife have been called out of town on a family medical emergency, and enlisted Buck to look after their three children while they're gone. But before he can drive from his cluttered studio apartment in the heart of Chicago out to the 'burbs, Uncle Buck needs his hat. Not just any hat: a sheepskin-lined bomber, replete with ear-flaps, the sort of topper that might look incredibly fresh on an original b-boy, but pushes the limits of credulity on a portly, middle-aged, pale-faced bumbler. Groping atop the closet shelf, Buck is for the moment unaware that that's where he's stored his bowling ball. And then, with glacial inevitability, everything starts to slide.

"There's all this crap in his closet, right?" says Matt Dike. "And then the bowling ball falls off the shelf, and right when it hits him on the head, we added the 808 kick. Oh my *gahhhhd*, it sounds incredible, so funny! Totally Hughes' idea."

After their agreeable initial meeting, the director sent a rough cut of the film over to Dike and Ross and left them alone for a couple of weeks to come up with music cues. Watching the movie on the tiny TV in Dike's apartment, the Delicious duo began slotting in their magic: a slinky instrumental based around Ben E. King's "Supernatural Thing" for the bar scene where Buck is read the riot act by his girlfriend Chanice (Amy Madigan); a humpbacked track meant to mimic the lurch and shudder of Buck's 1975 Mercury Marquis coupe belching down the highway; a specially extended rap-free edit of "Wild Thing" fit to function as Buck's personal theme. When Hughes, Dike, and Ross reconvened, the director listened approvingly to their work, then together they added drum machine hits to accentuate certain beats in the film, all the while cracking themselves up.

Released in theaters on August 16, 1989, *Uncle Buck* was a left turn for John Hughes. Not a turn into obscurity, but a further angle away from his established stock of ensemble teen flicks. A John Candy vehicle full of slapstick moments, the film also carries heavy undertones about the challenges of being a kid and the antipathies that build up inside a family. The depth of the belly laughs comes from the nuanced emotion that Candy, the actor, was capable of portraying. It doesn't hurt that the two younger Russell children are the absurdly adorable Maizy (Gaby Hoffman, greatest eyebrows ever) and Miles (hello world, it's Macaulay Culkin).

From a music perspective, *Uncle Buck* is unique in the John Hughes oeuvre. Unlike most of his films, which have a genre-specific musical identity, *Uncle Buck* deploys Delicious Vinyl hit songs and Dike/Ross-crafted incidental hip-hop beats alongside a smattering of R&B oldies and harmony novelties like LaVern Baker's "Tweedlee Dee", The Chordettes' "Mr. Sandman", and Big Joe Turner's "Lipstick, Powder And Paint". What unifies these sounds is an overall vibe of *fun*.

"I remember how Big John was fascinated with our set up and how we were doing stuff," says Michael Ross. "He loved the humor and vibe of 'Wild Thing.' When you think about it, it makes sense. He had this love for over-the-top slapsticky stuff and Tone's big hits had a lot of that. Tone could have been a great character in one of his movies. At the time, Matt and I were sort of over 'Wild Thing'. It was this monster that wouldn't die and we wanted to be known for doing other stuff. In retrospect, Big John was right on the money—it was the perfect fit."

Popular perception connects John Hughes, director, with the square-peg New Wave tunes that stuffed the hit soundtracks to his incisive teenage movies. But as John Hughes III explains, his father was a music fan of omnivorous tastes, from doo-wop to Delta blues to dub, with a record collection that included original hip-hop by Whodini, Mantronix, Beastie Boys ("he had their early single 'Cooky Puss'"), Malcolm McLaren ("he left 'Buffalo Gals' lying around, which was just the coolest shit ever"), and the crucial Mr. Magic *Rap Attack* comps. "My dad wasn't a teen music guy per se who only liked electro-pop," explains John Hughes III. "The reason that music is on the *Pretty In Pink* soundtrack is because that's what made sense for that movie. He was always trying to stay on top of the right stuff, and he was into everything. The reason he liked Delicious Vinyl was that it worked on the radio, but it was crazy. People didn't understand how cool it was! I don't know, maybe most people don't associate Delicious Vinyl with LA, but my father did. And he associated it with how cool LA could be."

"Dude, for a while there John Hughes was hanging out all the time!" says Matt Dike. "I guess he thought it was more fun than going to studio meetings."

The cool factor had been enough to seduce the Beastie Boys, who had relocated to LA in hopes of overhauling their frat-rap reputation. There's a chance that Hughes may have crossed paths with the Beasties at Dike's apartment—the other project that Dike was laboring over in early 1989 was tracks for the Beasties Boys' hash-drizzled sophomore opus, *Paul's Boutique*.

An element of Beastie intrigue colored a trip John Hughes III and his father took at the time to Tower Records on Sunset Boulevard. As John Hughes III remembers, "Every time we went to a record store, my dad bought a revolting amount of records. It was almost embarrassing going record shopping with him. So he was carrying a huge stack of CDs around Tower Records and we saw Mario there buying CDs too. I said, 'Dad, it's the guy from Delicious Vinyl!' My father went over to him and Mario had this huge stack of CDs. Parliament was on top, and my dad was like, 'Hey, what are you buying?' probably because he wanted to buy what Mario was buying. And Mario was like, 'Oh, Capitol's making me buy all these CDs. They're not happy with the crackles and scratches from

> "Apparently the audience went completely nuts when 'Wild Thing' started," says Matt Dike, "and Hughes was sitting there at the screening watching people lose their shit and was like, 'Oh, we've got to use that song. I've got to meet those guys.'"

the vinyl samples on the tracks, so we're using CDs to [re-source the samples on] *Paul's Boutique*.'" Mario looked depressed at having been sent on this errand.

Reminded of this, Mario Caldato, Jr. laughs: "I wasn't too bummed—it was a shopping spree on Capitol Records' dime. I've still got that Parliament CD. But yeah, we did re-source some of the samples from CD, but we sourced a lot from records, and a bunch of stuff from cassette tapes, too."

One morning Hughes appeared at Dike's door bearing coffee and doughnuts right as Matt was fiddling with a track based on Lightnin' Rod's "Sport". (The vintage break-beat is best known as the basis for Dismasters' bumptious 1987 single "Small Time Hustler"—it's often assumed, erroneously if understandably, that it's the Dismasters instrumental being used in *Uncle Buck*.) The Dike/Ross flip of the sample wound up soundtracking the scene where Buck goes looking for his errant niece Tia (Jean Louisa Kelly), who has fallen into the predatory clutches of a slimy suitor named Bug (Jay Underwood). The bassline kicks as Buck tracks down the teenagers by a bonfire in the woods, calling with terrifying jollity out the window of his trusty, rusty Mercury Marquis: "Just driving by for some ice cream! Maybe your Bug here can join us? We can talk about burying the hatchet! *You know what a hatchet is, don'tcha Bug?*"

⤜══⤛

The visit to Matt Dike's apartment proved a formative night in the life of John Hughes III, who calls it "the beginning of my adult bonding with my father." After completing high school in Illinois, the younger Hughes founded the progressive electronic label Hefty Records as an outlet for both his own music and that of groups like Savath & Savalas and Telefon Tel Aviv.

"That first night at Dike's, while Mike Ross and my father were talking, Matt brought me over to this huge pile of records he had on the floor. He pushed the records back, and was showing me that the floor was buckling because there were so many records. Matt thought that was funny." After young John told Matt he wanted to make music, "Dike told me, 'Get your father to get you an SP-1200, you'll love it!' He said, 'Get the soundtrack to *Car Wash*, that's all you need!' I still have that drum machine. It's my therapy piece, the one great piece of gear I know so well. I still use it.

"The amount of people who tell me they got to talk to my dad for 10 minutes and tell me it was life-changing, that's sort of how I felt about Matt." John Hughes III's voice catches with emotion. "When I lost my dad...when you have someone that special in your life, you take it for granted, he's just there. Something about losing my dad and thinking about that 15 minutes I had with Matt when he was giving me advice that put me on a path for something I was going to do for the rest of my life, it makes me grateful."

In the end, the pairing of John Hughes and Delicious Vinyl left at least one intriguing, unrealized project on the table: the creation of a joint venture called Delicious Pictures. Intimations of a post–*Uncle Buck* partnership came via an article titled "High-Flying Delicious Vinyl Craves Taste of Film Biz Success" in the December 10, 1990 issue of *Daily Variety*, with a quote from Michael Ross: "We've started a production company...we'll develop some story ideas with John Hughes." The first story idea came courtesy of Kevin Dolan, drummer for Echo and the Bunnymen knockoffs Abecedarians and a good pal of Dike and Ross. Growing up in Las Vegas alongside prodigal golfer and prodigious drinker Tommy Armour III (later a star on the PGA tour), Dolan had indulged in all the mischief Sin City had to offer.

"We discussed making a movie about Dolan's life as a kid in Las Vegas in the late '60s and '70s," explains Ross, "sort of a *Basketball Diaries/Dazed and Confused* vibe with young wild kids doing drugs, stealing shit, playing golf, trying to get laid against the backdrop of the Strip, with parents who worked in casinos and were never around. Hughes was really into it."

Kevin Dolan began working on the script, which Matt Dike remembers for one particular scene: "All these sort of burnout kids in Vegas are frying on acid and they go into the fountains outside the big casinos with rakes and pails and steal all the change that tourists have thrown in during the day. That would've looked great in a movie!"

"Dolan never finished the script," says Ross. "I think Big John's take was to make it a little more PG than the R vibe we felt it needed to be. I remember we were talking about how the movie should open, the father coming home from his night shift working at the casino, and he's taking a shower and John suggested that you see the father's butt through the mist of the shower door. When he said that, me and Matt sort of looked at each other and rolled our eyes like, *How corny!* We were such arrogant dummies." Ross laughs. "Think about it—John Hughes was giving us notes on a movie idea."

The so-called "Decade of Greed" was gaudily self-conscious about being "the '80s" as it was happening, and when it ended, an era ended with it. Although Delicious Vinyl experienced success in the 1990s with The Pharcyde, those madcap records were not produced by Mike Ross and Matt Dike, nor would they scale the chart summit that Tone Lōc and Young MC had. Shortly after the release of *Uncle Buck* and *Paul's Boutique*, Matt Dike moved out of his Santa Monica Boulevard apartment and into an Echo Park mansion where he has lived a peculiar existence of chosen seclusion ever since. In effect, when the 1980s ended, so did Dike's public persona.

In the '90s, John Hughes scripted the wildly successful *Home Alone* movies, but he is rightly perceived as an '80s director—a fact confirmed by many of the tributes that poured forth after his death, in August 2009, at age 59.

With *Uncle Buck*, John Hughes became a champion for hip-hop in Hollywood cinema, the first director to extensively integrate hip-hop into a hit film that was itself not expressly black or hip-hop oriented. That Dike, Ross, and Hughes never worked together again is a tantalizing footnote. Fortunately, there will always be the sound of a bowling ball falling on a funnyman's head. ✐

"Dude, for a while there John Hughes was hanging out all the time!" says Matt Dike. "I guess he thought it was more fun than going to studio meetings."

Peter Relic lives and writes in Los Angeles. His book-in-progress is Bust A Move! The Delicious Vinyl Story.

PAUL HORNSCHEMEIER
YOU'VE NEVER HEARD OF US
:
"WILDLIFE"

DAY THREE OF THE TOUR. TWO SHOWS SO FAR, TO MINISCULE CROWDS. WE'RE CRASHING ON FLOORS, EATING BADLY, SHARING TRIVIA ABOUT TERRIBLE MUSIC AND WORSE TV. EVERYTHING'S AS IT SHOULD BE.

EXCEPT TODAY WE KILLED A BIRD.

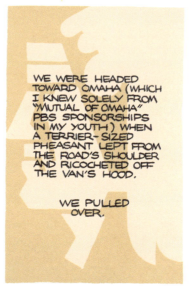

WE WERE HEADED TOWARD OMAHA (WHICH I KNEW SOLELY FROM "MUTUAL OF OMAHA" PBS SPONSORSHIPS IN MY YOUTH) WHEN A TERRIER-SIZED PHEASANT LEPT FROM THE ROAD'S SHOULDER AND RICOCHETED OFF THE VAN'S HOOD.

WE PULLED OVER.

THE BIRD WAS DEAD. I DON'T REMEMBER HOW WE FELT ABOUT IT.

I JUST KNOW I WAS THINKING ABOUT A RABBIT.

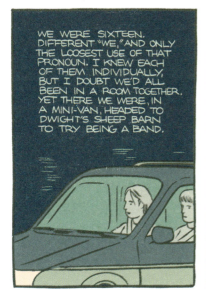

WE WERE SIXTEEN. DIFFERENT "WE," AND ONLY THE LOOSEST USE OF THAT PRONOUN. I KNEW EACH OF THEM INDIVIDUALLY, BUT I DOUBT WE'D ALL BEEN IN A ROOM TOGETHER. YET THERE WE WERE, IN A MINI-VAN, HEADED TO DWIGHT'S SHEEP BARN TO TRY BEING A BAND.

WHAT A BAND COULD MEAN, WE HAD ONLY THE MOST NASCENT AND DISPARATE OF IDEAS. ONLY DWIGHT PLAYED GUITAR. THE REST OF US CHOSE ROLES AT RANDOM. NONE OF US SHARED TASTE IN MUSIC OR KNEW HOW TO WRITE IT. THIS WAS BUILDING AN AIRPLANE FROM SPARE CAR PARTS, BLINDFOLDED.

WE JUST HAD THOSE TWO NECESSARY INGREDIENTS: PROXIMITY AND COMMON PURPOSE. WE ALL WANTED TO TRY THIS... *THING*.

SHIT! LOOK OU—

WE HELD A ROADSIDE FUNERAL. THEN WE TRIED MAKING MUSIC.

BOTH INSTITUTIONS WERE BEYOND US. WE DID OUR BEST.

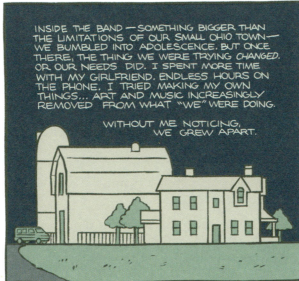

INSIDE THE BAND — SOMETHING BIGGER THAN THE LIMITATIONS OF OUR SMALL OHIO TOWN — WE BUMBLED INTO ADOLESCENCE. BUT ONCE THERE, THE THING WE WERE TRYING *CHANGED*. OR OUR NEEDS DID. I SPENT MORE TIME WITH MY GIRLFRIEND. ENDLESS HOURS ON THE PHONE. I TRIED MAKING MY OWN THINGS... ART AND MUSIC INCREASINGLY REMOVED FROM WHAT "WE" WERE DOING.

WITHOUT ME NOTICING, WE GREW APART.

THEN THEY TOLD ME THEY'D FOUND A REPLACEMENT. TURNED OUT THEY WERE TRYING SOMETHING NEW TOO.

IT WAS INEVITABLE, IN RETROSPECT. IT WAS THE SPEED OF IT THAT STUNG. THE NEWS SUDDENLY DELIVERED: YOU AND YOUR CHILDHOOD FRIENDS HAVE CHANGED, WILL EVENTUALLY MOVE ON TO OTHER EXPERIENCES, CITIES. BUT DOES IT MATTER IF THAT REALIZATION IS MORE PROTRACTED? MAYBE IT'S A TON OF BRICKS NO MATTER HOW IT FALLS.

A RABBIT.

A BIRD.

IT'D PROBABLY RESENT ME SEEING IT AS A METAPHOR. PROBABLY HAD A FAMILY, ETC.

WE GET BACK IN THE VAN.

WE KNOW EACH OTHER. WE SHARE MUSICAL TASTES.

THE GRAVITY OF PROXIMITY LONG BEHIND US, WE CHOSE ONE ANOTHER. WE'VE COLLECTIVELY MADE DECADES MORE CHOICES THAN THOSE FOUR KIDS IN OHIO STANDING AROUND A RABBIT.

BUT WE'RE STILL DRIVING, NOT KNOWING WHAT PART OF LIFE WILL CRASH INTO US NEXT. NOT HERE, OR IN A MYSTERIOUS LAND CALLED OMAHA.

The *Eternal* Otis

Respect Yourself: Stax Records and the Soul Explosion is the story of everyday people and their epic achievements. The "White Carnations" chapter, excerpted in this first installment of *The Pitchfork Review*, is the heart and guts of the first half of the Stax story. Otis Redding embodied Stax's open door policy and the Bar-Kays, raised and groomed by the Stax staff, were the promise of the company's future. Their demise is the first of three massive wounds, any one of which would seem fatal to a company. But the Stax story—always unpredictable—is far from over.

BY ROBERT GORDON

ILLUSTRATIONS BY PATCH KEYES

This was a prolific period for Stax, the success fueling the fires of creativity. There were hits from house regulars: William Bell—"Never Like This Before", "Everybody Loves a Winner", and "Eloise (Hang on in There)"; from Booker T. & the MG's—"My Sweet Potato", "Booker Loo", "Hip Hug Her", "Groovin'" (released by the MG's before the original by the Rascals, because Tom Dowd shared an Atlantic test pressing with them, and they cut it on the spot), and "Slim Jenkins' Place"; Carla recorded one of her career highlights, "B-A-B-Y", and also hit with her Otis duet, "Tramp", a session that proved so much fun they recorded a whole album together, *The King and Queen of Soul*.

Otis's hits included "My Lover's Prayer", "Fa-Fa-Fa-Fa-Fa (Sad Song)", and his incredibly innovative take on "Try a Little Tenderness", transforming a standard into a truly personal vision. "Tenderness" dates to the 1930s, and had been covered by Bing Crosby and Nina Simone, among many others. Phil Walden suggested the song, and before Otis played Phil his version, he told Phil, "It's a brand new song now." Sam and Dave's "I Can't Stand Up", a less-shouted, more nuanced vocal, was another in their run (a bigger hit abroad than in the U.S.), this one written by Stax's Homer Banks and Allen Jones, a break from the duo's Hayes and Porter hits.

Newly arrived Albert King, after making his presence known with "Laundromat Blues", released classics "Crosscut Saw" and "Born Under a Bad Sign". Eddie Floyd hit again with "Raise Your Hand", Mable John announced her arrival with "Your Good Thing (Is About to End)" and "Same Time, Same Place", and Johnnie Taylor got comfortable, hitting with "I Got to Love Somebody's Baby", "Little Bluebird", and "Ain't That Lovin' You (for More Reasons Than One)".

Stax expanded its publishing offices, taking over the neighboring bay to the west after the TV-repair service closed. David Porter was growing a team, and now they had a place with their own piano, where the business of writing and publishing could be managed. The glory spread beyond the artists. *Record World* magazine named Jim Stewart its outstanding record producer of 1967, and in early 1968, Jim announced an expansion into St. Louis, taking over office space and a studio there. He told *Billboard* that Stax was eyeing studio space in Atlanta too.

The thrill of the European tour was still hanging like a garland around the musicians when another call came, this time from the west. Promoters in California were planning the first rock and roll festival, modeled on successful jazz and folk festivals. Organizers in Monterey wanted Otis to help round out a lineup that included

The
ETERNAL
OTIS
Stax Family
BOOKER T AND THE MG's
Also Starring
ISAAC HAYES

"It's showmanship, it's artistry, it's love and affection, and that night in Monterey, California, it was contagious. The Love Generation caught Otis Redding."

established artists performing alongside relatively unknown British rock acts, upcoming psychedelic artists, and blues, jazz, and country artists. Jimi Hendrix, Janis Joplin, and The Who are among those who jump-started their careers at the Monterey Pop Festival. Otis was the only southern soul act invited, but one of the festival organizers, Andrew Oldham, who managed The Rolling Stones, was intent on exposing the Haight-Ashbury hipsters to this artist who had so strongly influenced his group. Any doubts about the show's potential were assuaged by the adamant endorsement of Jerry Wexler. Otis was still without a band and the MG's were committed to the studio, but they—and Jim Stewart—knew the West Coast exposure could be really helpful, so they happily obliged, the horns too. Everyone got their tour suits dry-cleaned and prepared to go west for the June 17, 1967, appearance. They were given the honor of closing the Saturday night of the festival.

Otis met the MG's and Mar-Keys there a day early, time enough to get refreshed and to review their show. "We had an afternoon rehearsal without amplifiers in a hotel room," says Duck, "just trying to remember what we'd done in Europe." The festival was in full swing, and Monterey was like a rainbow commune, an eye-opening, mind-blowing experience from the moment they arrived. "I stepped on the street in Monterey and it changed my life," Booker says, describing the place that won his heart and would eventually draw

him west to settle. "It was our first announcement that something new was happening in the United States. I had never seen people dress like that. For the first time I saw restaurants giving food for free. People were sharing hotel rooms and disregarding money. No police in the streets. Coming out of Memphis, it was a shock. History was changing at that moment, and we knew it."

"We'd seen hippies on television," says Wayne, "but we hadn't been around them, with the babies and flowers and headbands and doing all that love, dove, peace thing."

"The aroma," says Steve, referring to the prevalence of marijuana, "we weren't exposed to any of that yet. We were just little choirboys from Memphis." The cherubs found themselves at the dawning of the age of Aquarius. More than two years before Woodstock, this was the loudest announcement yet to mainstream America that there was more to rock and soul than girls screaming at The Beatles. Duck would promptly adopt the fashion, letting his hair and sideburns grow, getting a wide-brimmed hat and bell-bottoms. "There were 50,000 people there," says Wayne. "The biggest crowd we'd ever seen—three times bigger than my hometown. And they were all hippies."

On show day, the choirboys watched and waited. The Electric Flag, Moby Grape, Hugh Masekela—California was even further from Memphis than they imagined. Their set was to begin after Jefferson Airplane, who were hot with the recent singles "Somebody to Love" and "White Rabbit". By then, the show's schedule had fallen behind, and a light rain was beginning. The plan had been to give the hippies a proper soul revue, with the MG's warming up the crowd, then the horns joining them for a couple songs, a ramp-up to star time with Otis Redding. Festival organizers got in Otis's manager's ear, suggesting they cut the warm-up and go directly to the main event. Phil Walden didn't want to lose the crowd, and he bore down hard on the band to give up their set. When the Airplane finished, the rain caused a 15-minute delay and the tension backstage thickened. The audience, meanwhile, found the drizzle refreshing; the original plan held.

The MG's walked out wearing green mohair suits and Beatle boots, and in that audience at that time, *they* were the freaks: no one else looked like that. "We were doing our steps," says Wayne, "and we must have looked like a lounge act." Nothing may have looked right, but something was definitely working.

"Booker T. & the MG's took the stage with their little amps," says Jerry Wexler. "All day there'd been wild unin-

The fateful Friday, December 8, 1967. As the Bar-Kays prepare to leave Memphis for what will be their final tour, drummer Carl Cunningham (far left) laughs with neighborhood friends. One carries his gig clothes, dry cleaned.

hibited rock and roll and volume with 20-foot Marshall amps—all the wrong things about rock 'n' roll. And when the audience heard the real thing, they made the right responses. Next thing you know, you could hear the band and the groove. I found out one thing that night: when you got a loud crowd, play soft."

Filmmaker D.A. Pennebaker, the documentarian responsible for Bob Dylan's *Don't Look Back*, was there with a camera crew, and his film *Monterey Pop* (and the subsequent DVD of the entire Stax set) documents the crowd's reaction. After the warm-up there's a quick and low-key introduction from Tommy Smothers of the folk-comedy act the Smothers Brothers, and the audience reacts with mild applause. The horns play a galloping fanfare and Otis hustles onstage, his blue mohair suit contrasting with the band's matched green. Behind them is a 30-foot psychedelic display of swirls and strobing blobs. Moments into the first verse of "Shake", the Sam Cooke song performed at a trillion miles per hour, half the band drops out, leaving just Otis, Al Jackson, and Duck Dunn to carry the song—and they drive it, hauling the tens of thousands of people with them. Every audience likes dy-

namics, and Otis was winning them over. Aretha had just made a pop hit with her version of Otis's "Respect", and he next let the audience know where the song originated.

Catching his breath before the ballad—everyone needed a ballad after that fiery romp—he chatted with the audience, Booker's organ quietly evoking prayer time at the neighborhood church. Introducing "a soulful number," Otis asks, "This is the love crowd, right? We all love each other, don't we?" They assure him it is and they do. He can hear them, but he's not satisfied. "Am I right?" he screams, and they scream back at him affirmatively. "Let me hear you say *Yeah*, then!" And he hears them, a pregnant pause following, organ notes falling, a hole opening in the sky and the music outlining God's face. It's only a few seconds, but it's a world, too, and then Otis eases in: "I've been—" and he takes a breath, maybe two. It's as if he's finished his sentence. Subject, verb. The past tense is made present by the next words, framed by breaths, "loving you"—and the guitar begins to rise—"too lo-o-ng"—another breath—"to stop now." As fast as the other songs were, this one is that much slower. Did we rock your socks off? (Let me hear you say *Yeah*!) Well, now we're going to wrench your heart. (*Yeah!)* The horns stair-step up, soon to be answered by Booker's cascade down. Every note Steve plays is distinct—there's that much space. The verse is punctuated by three staccato notes, the whole band together, and Otis's body flails on each note. As if the song could get more amazing, Otis shares the intimacy of the group with the masses by casually turning toward the drummer and, totally unplanned, interrupts the song (without it feeling like an interruption) and says, "Can we do that one more time, Al, just like that?" and without pause or hesitation—the band is that tight—they give Otis three more notes. Each one fires like a rifle, and he flails and wails, then asks twice more to do it again—oh, oh, oh—and then eases into the rest of the song. It's showmanship, it's artistry, it's love and affection, and that night in Monterey, California, it was contagious. The Love Generation caught Otis Redding.

They were living the crossover moment, the cultural connection between the insular Southerners and progressive America—the white, record-buying hippies and the deep soul of Redding and the MG's. He followed with a reinterpretation of The Rolling Stones' "Satisfaction" that was familiar enough to keep the audience comfortable but also distinctly his own; the lead-guitar riff was played by the horns. The set and the night closed with "Try a Little Tenderness" rising from a ballad to a full-on soul maelstrom—"I don't want to go but I have to go y'all"—and when he leaves, the heavens open, a destiny manifest, a new audience that will leave the show and seek his records. Louis Armstrong crossed over, Sammy Davis Jr. crossed over, Sam Cooke crossed over, and finally, great God almighty, Otis Redding was reaching that fabled shore.

"After that," says Jim Stewart, "especially on the West Coast, his sales mushroomed." Otis's career had been a steady and constant ascension, a fire that continuously grew in both light and heat. Finally, it was raging.

Zelma Redding recollects him standing in the doorway after he made his way home. "He said, 'You just can't believe what happened.' He said, 'I blew them away.'" Zelma laughs. "Monterey was a highlight. Him walking in that door and looking with those big eyes, saying, 'I killed them.' He just knew he was on the right path."

Sam and Dave were also walking that path. Since hitting with "Hold On, I'm Coming", the duo had released "Said I Wasn't Gonna Tell Nobody", "You Got Me Hummin'", and "When Something Is Wrong with My Baby", all written by Isaac Hayes and David Porter and all top-ten R&B hits. From the European tour, their live version of Sam

"The festival was in full swing, and Monterey was like a rainbow commune, an eye-opening, mind-blowing experience from the moment they arrived."

Cooke's "Soothe Me" also hit the charts. They performed nearly three hundred shows a year, carrying a band that would soon grow to sixteen pieces—mostly horn players whose energetic moves with their gleaming instruments became solar flares radiating from these two stars. They were widely known as the greatest live act of all time.

Songwriters Hayes and Porter were also on an astral plane, merged into a single identity. Their songs seemed pulled from the ether wholly formed for listening enjoyment, but their channeling of the ordinary to create something extraordinary was in fact a laborious process requiring dedication, discernment, and discipline. "It's amazing how one little spark will ignite," Isaac says, explaining how they wrote the duo's next timeless hit. "'Soul Man' was written when there was a lot of racial unrest in this country. There was uprising in various cities, people burning buildings—Watts, Detroit. So I was watching TV and one of the news commentators said, 'If the black businesses write *soul* on the building, the rioters will bypass it,' and I thought about the night of the Passover in the Bible, blood of the lamb on the door, the firstborn is spared. And I realized the word *soul* keeps them from burning up their establishments. Wow, soul. Soul. Soul man. 'David, I got one!' So we started working on it and came up with 'Soul Man'."

Released in August of 1967, the song opens with Steve playing a (deceptively) simple two-string guitar lick, backed by a tambourine beat. But that restraint gives way to a playful horn line. As Sam's lead vocal kicks in, he's

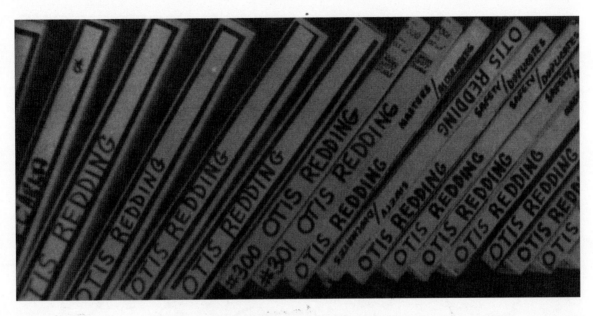

Part of the Otis Redding shelf at Stax.

nearly growling, singing of a daring love rescue. Each part is perfectly placed as the song progresses, a carousel of leads and hooks, none battling the other, each a support when not in the spotlight. The horns have applied all they've learned from Otis, alternating between complicated but catchy lines and bedrock foundations for the other instruments. Steve injects such exciting bluesy slide-guitar parts that Sam Moore can't contain himself during one of the choruses and, seeing him create these sounds by moving his Zippo lighter along the strings, Sam hollers out, "Play it, Steve!" Play it he does, they all do, all the way to the number-one spot on the R&B charts (where it stayed for seven weeks) and to number two on the pop charts. Race riots were occurring in Boston, New York, Chicago, and cities large and small across the country. "When 'Soul Man' becomes a national number one record," wrote *Rolling Stone* magazine at the time, "it indicates that a much more earthy, low-down kind of soul is beginning to get to white America."

On the heels of Monterey, Otis was ready to tour again, his management eager to capitalize on his success. The MG's were tethered to the studio, and he needed a band. He'd been hearing of the MG's protégés, the kids they'd been training and who'd had their own hit, but it wasn't till that spring that he got to hear them. On a visit to Memphis, he went with Carla Thomas and some other Stax artists to Beale Street, where the Bar-Kays were playing at the Hippodrome. "The Bar-Kays were doing their thing," recalls Carla Thomas, who'd accompanied Otis to the club. "We were all sitting at the table, and Otis said, 'Listen to those little boys!' He called them 'little boys.' 'Listen to those little boys! My goodness, they sound like tenfold.'"

The Bar-Kays could play the hits of the day as well as their own material (they were nearly done recording their first album, a mix of originals and cover songs). Guests began sitting in with the band, and Otis leapt at the opportunity. "When Otis got up there and we started playing behind him," says James Alexander, "he kept looking back. We were just teenagers, we had all this energy—boundless energy. And when we finished our performance, he just kept saying, 'I like this band.'" He mentioned going on the road, an idea that appealed to these "little boys" much more than attending school. "He said he would get us a tutor so we could travel and be his band," James continues, "but our parents banded together and said, 'We're not going to let these kids go until they finish high school.' At that time, all of the Bar-Kays except for me were in the twelfth grade. I was in the eleventh grade. And it was very clear that we was going to end up playing with Otis Redding."

"Oh, Otis loved those kids so much," says his widow, Zelma Redding. "One of the reasons for getting a new, bigger plane was so the Bar-Kays could tour with him

and he could get them home on Sunday night or Monday morning so they could go to school. They was his babies. That's exactly what the Bar-Kays were. And they had so much talent."

Four of the five Bar-Kays threw their high school graduation caps in the air and then all of them, including rising senior James Alexander, boarded a plane that very night bound for New York and a series of gigs at the Apollo. They'd had no rehearsal; Otis had told them which records to learn, and in the dressing room before the first show, they discussed the gig. "The night of graduation," says James, "we took a flight to New York—a group of guys that have never been no more than a 50-mile radius in all directions of Memphis, Tennessee. That whole thing that Stevie Wonder says—'skyscrapers and everything'—we're just looking all around." The bill had other soul stars on it, and between sets of the whole revue, the Apollo ran a feature film. "The Apollo audience is tough," James continues. "They had four or five shows a day, starting from like 12:45 pm. We didn't have but one uniform at the time, so we would wear that uniform all day. Parents would drop their kids in the morning and there

wasn't no such thing as turning over the house. You'd ask the crowd, 'How y'all doing this evening?' Nobody would respond. If somebody has been there since a quarter to one, they might answer, 'When you going to change clothes?' We were there for 10 days, and before we left, we won them over."

"The last day at the Apollo, we did one of the best shows of my life," says trumpeter Ben Cauley. "As the group played, Otis called James Brown onto the bandstand, and we were doing 'Papa's Got a Brand New Bag'. We was playing some stuff there that I couldn't explain to you. But Otis was stepping, James was stepping, and we started stepping right with them. 'One thing's for sure,' Otis said, 'I don't care if y'all are stepping because y'all be playing your behinds off!' We were in full bloom. Whatever we needed, it just opened up."

That summer, Otis toured heavily with the Bar-Kays. He'd upgraded to a twin-engine Beechcraft private plane; it held eight people, but they were a ten-person entourage: Otis, the pilot, two valets, and six Bar-Kays. They worked out a rotation system. "When we got to each city," explains James Alexander, "we would always rent two vehicles. The two not on the private plane would drop the group at the hangar, then return the rental vehicles and take a commercial flight." They played all over the continent, including a show at the Expo 67 World's Fair in Montreal, Canada, on July 4, and a week in San Francisco at the Basin Street West that James recalls as among their best gigs. The Bar-Kays pushed Otis hard; he'd been developing a serious hoarseness, and it worsened. When a doctor found polyps on his vocal cords, surgery was required. The operation would risk that he'd never sing again, but if he didn't have it, he was guaranteed to lose his voice. Some of the Bar-Kays had enrolled for the fall semester of college in Memphis, so there was a natural break around Labor Day. The convalescence required six weeks of total silence, and Otis decided to throw a last party. He was having a swimming pool installed at the Big O Ranch, so he planned a huge gathering there for Labor Day weekend. He set up a stage and featured Sam and Dave, Arthur Conley, the Bar-Kays, and others. They cooked five pigs and two cows, and guests arrived on buses from Atlanta. Otis didn't perform, worn out by the summer's travels, but he was a gracious host. "He was so tired he was just sitting there out in the middle of the front yard," Zelma said. "He spoke to everybody but he just couldn't move."

For the first time in this constant climb for success, Otis would have a few weeks off. His children were five, four, and three, and he'd taste bonding time with them. He'd have quiet time with Zelma, from whom he'd grown distant by the constant travel. And he'd have time with his thoughts—to be creative, to reflect on where he'd come from and where he was going. He was 26, and the past five years had been a blur. He'd be able to consider his relationships: with his manager, with his record company, with his wife. After Labor Day, he went under the knife, and the Bar-Kays went back to school.

Otis wouldn't know the surgery's results until six weeks had passed. If he tested his voice, he could do irreparable damage. Strict silence, doctor's orders. He couldn't even shout for joy when the October issue of the British magazine *Melody Maker* named him top male vocalist; he'd dethroned Elvis from the position the King had held for ten years. In the quiet, he wrote new material. Instead of having to snatch an hour after sound check, or pull out the guitar before going to bed, he could really focus on songwriting. "He dissected the *Sgt. Pepper* album," says manager Phil Walden. "I'd get him Bob Dylan albums and stuff like that. It made him much more conscious of the importance of lyrics."

When he returned to the doctor, the results were very good indeed. Given clearance to resume his career, his voice quickly resumed strength. With a mixture of excitement and trepidation, he booked time at Stax for the end of November and beginning of December, more than two weeks—time enough to polish some songs with Steve Cropper and to record a batch of new material.

"Otis was so busy on the road we could hardly get time to do any sessions with him," says Jim. This was going to be different.

"Otis called me from the airport," Steve remembers. He'd just landed in Memphis, and he was excited. "He was coming in to write, and then we were gonna set up the sessions based on what we'd written. He said, 'I gotta show you this song.' He said, 'I'm coming right down to the studio.'" When he walked in, he told Steve to get his "gut-tar" (as he pronounced it); Steve kept an acoustic Gibson B-25 at the studio. Otis wrote songs in open tuning, so Steve tuned to open E. "He started singing this 'Dock of the Bay'," says Steve. "He had the intro and most of the first verse. I helped him with, I think, 'I left my home in Georgia, headed for the Frisco bay,' and then I wrote the bridge with him."

They quickly recorded the song. (Steve remembers doing it early in the sessions; Jim says it was the very last song.) "We had been trying to find something that Otis could sing that would be a crossover hit," Steve continues. "We tried ballads, from 'A Change Is Gonna Come' to 'Try a Little Tenderness'. We came close, but we didn't really have that record that leaves rhythm and blues and starts going up the pop charts, being played by popular demand. The day we recorded 'Dock of the Bay', we looked at each other and said, 'This is our hit, we got it.'"

Jim Stewart, harking back to his first session with Otis, wasn't terribly impressed by "Dock of the Bay". The song was unusual for Otis, and didn't strike Jim like "I've Been Loving You Too Long" or "Try a Little Tenderness".

In fact, "Dock of the Bay" has none of the trademark Otis Redding characteristics. There's not the rambunctious energy, there's no growling vocals, it's not a ballad that aches. Rather, it's introspective and contemplative, a sudden synthesis of The Beatles and Bob Dylan by a soul singer. He'd been captivated by the recently released *Sgt. Pepper* album—but the song is hardly derivative of The Beatles. It conveys a new worldliness, an ability to present the ultimate sophistication, which is simplicity. It's a leap in the way that Otis's first session

OTIS REDDING

PROMOTIONAL PHOTOGRAPH.

was, when he went from imitating Little Richard to establishing his own ballad style, walking through a door he hadn't previously the confidence, nor the artistic development, to enter.

During those couple weeks in Memphis, Otis recorded and sang, sang and recorded. "Hard to Handle" hit the tape. They cut the Five Royales' "Tell the Truth", Zelma's "I've Got Dreams to Remember", the propulsive "Love Man". Things kept getting better. "Before the operation, he couldn't sing all night," Steve explains. "His voice would break up. But after, he just kept going. We were up till 6 am one morning." His post-surgery voice sounded so much stronger and warmer that they dug up multitrack tapes from prior sessions and replaced the older vocals. Over the two weeks, they cut nearly four albums' worth of material.

On Friday, December 8, they took a break. That weekend, Otis was to perform three shows with the Bar-Kays—Nashville, Cleveland, and then Madison, Wisconsin—and the MG's (with David Porter on vocals) were going out Saturday to play Indiana State University. "Otis stuck his head in the studio before leaving," says Steve, "and said, 'See ya on Monday.'"

Otis's Friday-night gig in Nashville ended early, so at his suggestion they left for Cleveland right away, giving them a chance to catch a bit of the O'Jays and the Temptations at Leo's Casino, the same Cleveland club

they were booked into. It was a treat for the band. They did the *Upbeat* TV show that afternoon and when they played Saturday night, "It was just unbelievable," says James, "the crowd response was just unbelievable."

On Sunday, James Alexander and roadie Carl Sims dropped the band at the hangar. It was midday in Cleveland and cold. Ben Cauley remembers that Carl Cunningham asked for the plane to be turned on so the cabin could warm up. The attendant "told us he couldn't crank it up because the battery was kind of low," says Ben. "He said he'd rather have the pilot do it. We looked at each other, as young fellows do, and said, 'The battery's low?' Five minutes after that it got started—but we were still thinking about that. Then we took off going to Madison with no problems."

There were no direct flights to Madison, so James and Carl caught a plane to Milwaukee. Otis's pilot would shuttle them to Madison for the 6:30 gig, the first of two at the club that night. In Milwaukee, they waited, and they waited some more. "This was not like them," says James. "We started calling around and calling around. We called the hangar and couldn't find them. Two or three hours passed and we still didn't know anything."

The private plane's flight had gone smoothly enough that most of the guys were catching a nap. The pilot was given clearance to land at 3:25 pm, four miles from Madison. Visibility was hampered by low cloud cover, dense at 100 feet. "We were three minutes from landing," says Ben Cauley, "and then it crashed. I remember waking up because I couldn't breathe. The engines sounded real loud and I had a funny spinning sensation of falling through space. I thought the plane had hit an air pocket. [Saxman] Phalon was sitting next to me and said, 'What's that, man?' And he looked out the window. Now, what he saw, I couldn't tell you, but I do remember, he says, 'Oh no.' And I turned to say something to him, but I couldn't because I couldn't breathe. I unbuckled my seatbelt. I was going to tell them to do the same thing, but I wasn't fast enough. I'm bumping around. Mentally, I wanted to tell them to. But I had done mine. This may have saved my life."

The low battery was affecting the instrument panel and perhaps the engines, while the pilot's judgment was hampered by the clouds and his inexperience in cold weather, the temperature intensified by the bitter lake below. A Lake Monona resident heard the peculiar engine sound, so loud and low, and stepped outside to see the plane appear through the cloud cover—and crash into the water. He called authorities. They would arrive

54

"We were three minutes from landing," says Ben Cauley, "and then it crashed. I remember waking up because I couldn't breathe. The engines sounded real loud and I had a funny spinning sensation of falling through space."

in seventeen minutes. Upon impact, the plane's fuselage ripped open, ejecting Cauley and the others.

Otis was seated in the front, next to the pilot. He'd become an airplane enthusiast, and after some informal training, the pilot sometimes let him fly. But he'd stayed up late with the other guys, and he was also taking a nap. "Otis was sitting directly in front of me in the copilot's seat," Ben continues. "I didn't hear him say a word. Didn't see him do a thing. The next thing I remember is bobbing up in the water holding onto this cushion. I was on top of all this water. And then I saw Phalon coming up after me, and Ronnie, and some of the cats come up—Carl [Cunningham], I saw Carl. And I said, 'What in the world are we doing?' At that time, my mind was really fogged up. And the only thing I could think was, 'We're in the wrong place. We're in the wrong place'. I'll never forget that.

"I was in the water about a good 22 minutes. And I was cold out there. I had on my winter shoes and I remember my right shoe was on. And I had my trench coat on. And, I was bleeding in my head, I didn't realize that. And I was cold. I was shaking. I saw little bits of ice floating around in the water.

"I was the only one who couldn't swim. I was holding the airplane seat in my hand. Do you know, I lost it in the water, the airplane seat? I saw Ronnie come out. I'll never forget that. Ronnie came up and he was hollering for help. And I was saying, 'Ronnie, hold on man. I'm trying to get over to you.' I was trying to get to him, and the more I

tried to get to him, this airplane seat was slipping out my hand. And then finally, it slipped out of my hand and at that point, I said, 'Oh no.' I knew I was next because I didn't have nothing, and then another seat cushion came straight to me.

"I saw Carl come out of the water. He didn't say anything. I saw [Otis's valet] Matt come up on the other side. And then, for a while, nobody was there. They had floated away or drowned. And, I felt like—I knew I was next." Cauley remembers that he'd begun slipping into the water, fighting to stay afloat, the chaotic and panicked efforts of a drowning man. "I laid there one time and then I came back up and said, 'I'm all right.'" He'd been in the water for 17 minutes, his body moments from severe hypothermia, and when he felt like he was going down for the last time, "Someone just lifted me up. When they got me aboard the boat, I couldn't talk at all. I saw them bringing the others in and that's when I stopped talking. When they got Jimmy—just think about it, what I saw. I tightened up. I could not talk. I said, 'What is this?' But I couldn't talk." The images in his head are dreamlike, a nightmare of confusion and shock. "There was this thing over all our heads, including me too. They didn't want me to see what really had happened. And I was trying to get to them to help them, to see if everything was all right. And they just kept constantly pushing me back down, told me to lay down. 'Are you all right?' And, I said, 'I'm all right.'"

Ben, husband and father to a nine-month-old, was taken to a hospital. "I remember the coroner told the nurse and two of the doctors to stay around my bedside because I was in shock. I didn't know what shock was. But I knew how I was feeling. I couldn't talk. And I was scared because Jimmy and them was gone. And when I came back around, I realized what really happened to me." What really happened was that the dead bodies of guitarist Jimmy King and pilot Dick Fraser had been pulled from the lake, and there was a frantic search for the others as nightfall closed in. He remembers, "I kept asking, 'Are they all right?' And this guy just looked at me and said, 'Well, son, you're the only one alive.' Once he said that, I couldn't talk. I'd never been that way before in my life. I was shaking all over."

James Alexander and Carl Sims were still waiting for their ride to the gig. "Then some authorities came to Milwaukee to pick us up," says James, "and they said, 'The plane went down.' They didn't have any details other than the plane had gone down." Slowly, more information came in. First they were told that everyone had died, and then later that Ben had survived. "We got to Madison, we went to talk to—to see Ben in the hospital and he was in a state of shock. He was just laying there with his eyes open. He didn't really know he was there at that point."

James Alexander, 17 years old, had the grisly task of identifying the bodies. "I was numb," he says. "That Sunday night, late, we identified two people. Just a strange thing to do, especially when all these guys were your friends and you grew up with them, and then here you have to go and identify them in a morgue. That's tough."

Jim Stewart got a call that Sunday evening from Joe Galkin, the traveling promotions man who'd brought Otis to his attention a short five and a half years earlier. Galkin told him to turn on the television, and Jim absorbed the news with the rest of the world. He remembered that last session, and an unusual feeling he'd had. "I had gone to my office," Jim says, "and I knew Otis was getting ready to leave. I had the feeling that I must tell Otis good-bye. I had never felt that way before. Otis would come in and everything would be hectic and then he'd leave and I'd never think anything about it. I don't know if you believe in premonitions, but if you listen to the lyrics on 'Dock of the Bay', it's kind of scary if you relate that to the events that happened. And I was never able to say good-bye."

The MG's were trapped by the weather in the Indianapolis airport. "We had missed our connection," Steve remembers. "There was an icy runway. And I know we made the comment that if we could get a hold of Otis's pilot, he'd come get us out of here. David Porter called home to let his wife know. We didn't all want to spend the same dime, so he was going to ask his wife to call our wives. And he came back, just—'What's wrong?' And he'd just found out. His wife heard on the radio that Otis's plane had gone down."

"We had just come from a wedding of one of our very good friends," says Carla Thomas. "We had gotten home and we were jiving and joking about it. And we just happened to turn on the TV, and we were in this elated mood. And then they said, 'Bulletin.' Just, *boom*. 'Plane belonging to Otis Redding . . .' And I knew that the kids were with him. They were traveling together. And, what I did? I just put my hands in my ear. I didn't even hear the rest of it. Mother and I were in there together, so after the bulletin went off, I looked at her. She looked at me. And I said, 'What did they say?' I wanted to get it secondhand. And then she told me."

"I was in the kitchen, the phone rang," says Wayne Jackson. It was his horn partner, Andrew Love, call-

ing. "He said, 'Did you hear about Otis?' When you hear those words, you know something really bad's happened. I said, 'No. I hadn't been listening to the radio today.' And he said, 'They're all gone.' I said, 'What do you mean, "gone?"' He said, 'They're gone. They all went in the lake up in Wisconsin.' And we stood there, just silence, nothing but static in the air."

Silence. Static. "And that's the way I thought my life would be with no Otis in it. He was such a predominant force in our lives and we'd learned so much about being energetic and having a great time, the joy that you feel playing music with him. It was really hard to get a hold of the fact that he was gone and would never be back."

JIMMY KING, AGE EIGHTEEN. GUITARIST.
CARL CUNNINGHAM, AGE EIGHTEEN. DRUMMER.
PHALON JONES, AGE NINETEEN. SAXOPHONE.
RONNIE CALDWELL, AGE NINETEEN. ORGAN.
MATTHEW KELLY, AGE SEVENTEEN. VALET.
RICHARD FRASER, AGE TWENTY-SIX. PILOT.
OTIS REDDING, AGE TWENTY-SIX. STAR.

Such a tragedy brings out the crass essence of a commercial enterprise like a record label. Steve remembers, "We got a call from Atlantic saying, 'We've got to rush something out immediately. What have you got?' And I immediately said, 'We need to put our hit out.' The difficulty was not the fact that it had to be done real quick. The difficulty was—they hadn't even found Otis's body yet." Cropper threw himself into the project, a way to block all other thoughts from his mind. He added electric guitar, seagulls, and the sound of waves. He went in early and mixed all night. "I handed it to a flight attendant, who flew it to New York and handed it to a representative from Atlantic. Trying to work on something like that when you don't even know where one of your closest friends is, is difficult."

Otis's body wasn't found until later on Monday, when Carl Cunningham was also retrieved. The ongoing search was hampered by the chill of the water. "Police skin divers said they were unable to remain in the 30–40 degree water longer than fifteen minutes at maximum," *Sepia* magazine reported. When Otis was brought up, he was still buckled into his seat, his eyes closed. "He looked," said a witness, "as if he was taking a nap." Four thousand five hundred people overflowed the Macon Municipal Auditorium's 3,000 seats for Otis's funeral. The hour-long service was quiet and solemn. Joe Simon sang "Je-

The death of the Bar-Kays reached deep into the Memphis community.

sus Keep Me Near the Cross", and midway through Zelma broke down, wailing and stamping her feet in sorrow. Decorum was broken only when James Brown exited the building, mobbed by teenagers who pounced on his car; when it tried to follow the hearse, their weight caused the tires to spin, blue smoke rising. Otis was buried at the Big O Ranch, in view of his kitchen window.

The funerals for Cunningham, King, and Kelly were held together on Sunday the 17th, a week after the crash. Aptly, a heavy rain descended from a gloomy Memphis sky. Nearly 3,000 mourners filled Clayborn Temple AME Church, and the speakers included Estelle Axton and the principal of Booker T. Washington High School who said, "We are witnessing a phenomenon of life, in which the evening sun of their lives has gone down while it is still morning." During the service, word spread that divers had just found Phalon Jones. The line of cars leading to the cemetery ran over a mile long. The four African-American Bar-Kays are buried alongside each other at New Park Cemetery. Ronnie Caldwell, whose body was not recovered until Wednesday, was buried on the 22nd in a family plot.

"That next week I went to Stax," says Cauley, where a wreath of white carnations hung on the door. "It was like going back home, because we put so much into Stax. It

was part of us. We used to sit on the floor many nights and practice, rehearse and play shows together. And Miz Axton was there with us. Miz Axton was like our mama. The Bar-Kays could do no wrong because of Miz Axton. She came in and hugged me."

"Otis was not only an artist; he was a dear friend," says Jim. "He stayed at my home many times when he would come to town. It was a great loss, so much talent that we never got to explore. He was just beginning."

"Everybody was walking around staring at their feet for two months after that," says Marvell Thomas. "There was true sadness at that place. I didn't know Otis nearly as well as a lot of the other people did, but I certainly felt his loss. You would walk in the door—Stax was usually a happy, peppy place, there was conversations in the hallways and songwriters over here and a demo going—that all stopped. It was quiet like a mausoleum. Everybody was very sad and very introspective. And strictly from a business standpoint, Stax Records lost its biggest act. So they felt it psychologically, emotionally, and in their pocketbook."

"About a month or two after the plane crash," remembers Don Nix, "here comes a UPS truck with all these boxes. They were all warped and somebody come dumped them in the lobby. It was Carl's drums. They'd been at the bottom of that lake all that time. And everybody just sighed. We were getting over it, and I remember how that made me feel. 'Cause everyone was friends—a neighborhood. It was guys that cared about each other." ✐

As a writer and filmmaker Robert Gordon has focused on the American South—its music, art, and politics. Gordon's first book, It Came From Memphis, *careens through the 1950s, '60s, and '70s, riding shotgun with the weirdos, winos, and midget wrestlers. In 2003, Gordon published the definitive biography of blues great Muddy Waters. His Stax documentary,* Respect Yourself, *co-directed by Morgan Neville, was broadcast on PBS in 2007. And most recently, Gordon won a Grammy Award as a writer of the essay in the 2010 boxed set,* Keep An Eye On the Sky, *about the band Big Star. He lives in Memphis, Tennessee with his wife and two children.*

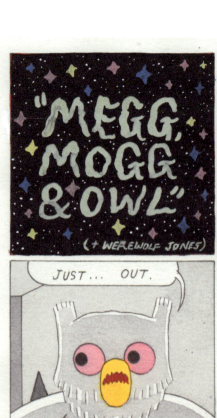

HE WALKS AMONG US

BY JESSICA HUNDLEY

ILLUSTRATIONS BY STERLING TEXAS

AN INTERVIEW WITH GLENN DANZIG

L odi, New Jersey is what you might expect, an East Coast working class burg, not many miles from New York City, but a world away in spirit. This is a static place—vinyl siding and rusted iron, a pocked sidewalk wet with rain outside the Satin Dolls Strip Club. The whole town seems caught in the murky amber of a dead-end era.

Growing up in Lodi, in the 1960s and 1970s, Glenn Allen Anzalone spent most of his time trying to find ways to escape. He read voraciously: Edgar Allan Poe and Baudelaire, stacks of superhero comics, and dusty tomes on the occult. He stayed up watching late-night B-horror and sci-fi flicks, like *Plan 9 From Outerspace* and *Vampira*. He collected animal skulls and drew dark, fantastical worlds in spiral-bound notebooks. He turned up the volume on the vinyl roar of Black Sabbath and Blue Cheer and Howlin' Wolf. Glenn also taught himself to play piano and electric guitar and started singing with an enviable range and a lusty, swaggering sort of voice, styled after Jim Morrison and Elvis Presley. He played in and fronted a series of local dirt bag metal bands, acts with names like Talus and Whodat and Boojang.

By age 11, Glenn was jamming in his basement, smoking grass, guzzling booze, and stirring up trouble. By 15, he was sober. And by 18, he had finally found his way out, leaving the confines of suburban Jersey to study at NYU's Tisch School of the Arts and the New York Institute of Photography. Soon after, he started his own band, The Misfits, whose name he lifted as an homage to the John Huston film of the same name, starring Clark Gable, Montgomery Clift, and Marilyn Monroe (the screenplay was penned by Arthur Miller, Monroe's husband at the time). The music he wrote for them would serve as the culmination of all that had obsessed him in Lodi: the books and movies and songs that had helped him make his great escape.

The Misfits were comic-book, horror-film heroes, bent on castrating the swollen ego of commercial rock radio. They pumped iron and flexed muscle and spit in the face of convention. They ate babies, drank wolf's blood, and worshipped at the altar of a dark lord. Their logo, a grinning, menacing skull, based on a villain from a 1940s Republic Pictures serial, has become, nearly 40 years later, a universal signifier of defiant nonconformity.

With The Misfits, and his subsequent bands, Samhain and Danzig, Glenn created an enduring cultural aesthetic, an iconic sound and vision that encompasses heavy metal, punk rock, horror, gore, Satanism, sci-fi, fantasy, and post-apocalyptic glee.

Today, Glenn Allen Anzalone, or Glenn Danzig, as he is better known, has finally, truly, escaped the bonds of

Lodi, and of the mundane and the mediocre. At 58, he has managed to build both a music and comic book empire, all while remaining an enduring outsider, working through much of his career without major label support or promotion.

He built his audience the old fashioned way, by recording and touring consistently, playing live shows that, over the years, attracted a voracious army of loyal fans. Many of his early contemporaries, such as Black Flag and Metallica, count themselves among his legions of fans. The latter helped to introduce The Misfits to a wider audience through their 1987 covers album, *The $5.98 E.P.: Garage Days Re-Revisited*. Metallica's guitar-shred versions of The Misfits tracks "Last Caress" and "Green Hell" are credited with pulling Glenn's first band out of obscurity, and also for introducing his work to Def Jam founder and producer extraordinaire Rick Rubin.

Rubin would go on to collaborate on Danzig's acclaimed, self-titled debut, releasing the album in 1988 on his label, Def American Recordings. The combination of Glenn's wailing tenor and bluesy, unrelentingly heavy riffs, along with Rubin's meaty production, resulted in a certified gold record. It remains the band's best-selling album to date.

Over the next 25 years, Danzig, both the band and the man, would continue to gain momentum, despite legal battles with former Misfits members and Glenn's bristly, short-tempered reputation when dealing with bookers, venues, and the music press.

His public conflicts are legend. There was the now notorious 2004 live show, where Glenn was hit in the face and knocked-out cold, on camera, by the frontman of a band called North Side Kings. The moment lives on in YouTube infamy. In 2011, citing crappy weather and a bad cold, Glenn hit the stage at Austin's Fun Fun Fun Fest 45 minutes late and played an abbreviated set to an increasingly angry crowd. In 2012, at Bonnaroo, Glenn was filmed attempting to start a fight with a particularly pushy photographer.

But the fact that Glenn Danzig is pissed off and doesn't mind throwing a punch (or taking one) shouldn't come as a surprise to anyone who knows his history, or his music. Danzig considers his anger an asset, and it is this inner wrath that has, in large part, fueled his creativity. His music and his art are a direct expression of his ire. His is a long-held disdain, both for music industry conventions and societal norms.

Danzig, the band, celebrated 25 years in September 2013 by playing a series of sold-out shows that included peace-keeping cameos from members of both The Misfits and Samhain, and a "greatest hits" set list featuring songs from all three of Glenn's revolutionary acts. His comic book company sells adult-themed fantasies to readers around the globe. And, as long-time director of his own music videos, the multi-talented artist is now focused on making the leap to the big screen.

Glenn Danzig not only escaped, he endured. For the first issue of *The Pitchfork Review*, we caught a Danzig show and talked with him about his self-created, four-decade-long musical and visual legacy.

Pitchfork: I was blown away by the range of ages at the show the other night. Can you talk about how you first formed a musical identity for yourself as a kid?

Glenn Danzig: The reason I started The Misfits in my basement was that I was just frustrated with music in general and what was going on with music at the time. All the bands that had come out of the 1960s were sell-outs and playing some of the worst, middle-of-the-road music ever at that point. And there was this whole system in place that kept perpetuating this idea of: "We need more of this now. We play this on the radio. We need more of this sound." It was a sound that was not so rebellious. It was very pedestrian—and the kind of music that was bought and sold on the radio. Mainstream radio wanted more of that sound, and that was really what spurred the punk movement, if you want to call it a musical revolution. I guess it really was. We wanted to change shit. We hated those bands, we wanted to do something different. When I tell you that I really hated Journey and Foreigner, to this day, I HATE those bands with a passion. I can't fucking stand them. The same thing with disco. It was like a fight against that mediocrity. It was like a war. Because as you must know, initially, no one would give punk the time of day. Naysayers said we were just kids, we couldn't play our instruments, we had no talent, etc. But, in those one- or two-minute songs we crafted, we packed more energy and excitement than what you could get on an entire album by one of those crappy bands I just mentioned. And those bands have their fans. They're just not my fans. And it was more than just the music. It was sociological at the same time. We didn't want to think like that. We didn't want to dress like that. It was like, "I'm not doing that." No one understood. *(CONTINUED ON PAGE 67)*

RICK RUBIN

*A*t first, Rick Rubin and Glenn Danzig may seem an odd couple. One, a bearded, big-bellied recording guru known for pioneering and popularizing hip-hop, the other, a prickly, iron-pumpin' Dark Angel of doom metal. But the two legends' roots run far and deep, twisted up together in the East Coast scene of the 1980s. In high school, Rubin fronted an NYC punk band called The Pricks, performing at some of the same clubs where Danzig was already playing it hard and fast.

By the time Rubin first saw a Danzig show, in 1986, he had guided hip-hop into the mainstream through his work with acts like the Beastie Boys and was about to begin a long and fruitful relationship with a young band called Slayer. On the advice of friends (rumored to be Metallica), Rubin

went to check out Danzig play—and was immediately hooked.

By 1988, Glenn had signed to the producer's new label, Def American Recordings, and with Rubin at the boards, released a now legendary, self-titled debut. Two years later saw the duo release Danzig II: Lucifuge, *and in 1992,* Danzig III: How The Gods Kill *and finally, in 1994,* Danzig 4.

By this time, the relationship between musician and producer began to deteriorate, dueling personalities and artistic temperaments causing the partnership to eventually implode. After years of bad blood, it slowly evolved again, to the friendship's current state of profound and mutual respect.

We talk to Rubin about his dear old friend Glenn.

When did you first hear about Glenn? Do you remember the first time you saw him play?

I saw The Misfits play at the Ukrainian Home on 2nd Avenue in New York and also at The Ritz. He was amazing from day one.

What about his work did you connect to initially?

First his singing and songwriting. Then as a bad-ass visual artist.

What made you want to collaborate with him musically?

I respected his songwriting and I thought we could make better records together than the ones he was making with Samhain at the time.

Glenn mentions you have a lot in common in terms of film and music tastes. What are some of your shared favorites?

We both like Ric Flair and Bill Medley.

What was your process like in the studio together and how did that evolve?

Glenn always had strong opinions but was open to collaborate with me. We tried all kinds of things to make the songs as good as they possibly could be, and we were more often than not in sync on what was best.

When working with someone like Glenn, what do you feel is necessary to bring to the table in terms of creative collaboration?

Nothing. We could openly discuss anything—that's what a good collaboration is, and we both wanted the other to love it as much as the other.

Why do you think the work you've done with him remains so relevant?

He's a great artist and an iconic figure. There is only one Glenn Danzig. Nobody even approaches him in his lane.

(CONTINUED FROM PAGE 65) *Rolling Stone* magazine certainly didn't understand it, and neither did *Circus* or any of these magazines that were out there at the time. Nobody understood it really, except the people who got it and went to the shows. Now, in retrospect, it's like the blues. We got no respect, we had to form and play our own circuit that we created, and now almost 40 years later, people are ripping us off left and right and never giving credit to the people they stole this shit from. It's just like the blues.

You say it was a sociological movement and it really was: with The Misfits, you were creating not only music, but a completely new aesthetic—one that encompassed everything you loved in pop culture, old horror movies, comic books. Looking back, is that how you remember it 35 years later?

Well, all those things we liked were considered trash at the time. B movies, in particular, were considered crap, and you were supposed to go see the new John Travolta movie if you went out to a theater. You know what I mean? Hollywood was stuffing crappy movies down everyone's throat and rarely would you see a good horror movie really, until later on. Until people like David Cronenberg redefined what the horror movie was. Until *Scanners* was number one as an independently made movie, people couldn't care less about horror. They only cared about the dollar. That's how all these movie studios are now and were back then.

Do you think it's better now or worse?

I think it's exactly the same. The only thing that's maybe better now is that classic rock radio stations are less powerful now, and there is more metal on mainstream radio. That's okay, but that means the more metal that gets played on the radio, the more the radio suits are going to define metal by what sells and what doesn't, instead of what's good. Through much of my career, I never relied on radio, I never relied on MTV. The fans I have—the people you saw at the show the other night—that's all from hard work, and from dealing directly with the audience, the people that come to the shows and buy the records. It's from taking our live show out on the road. There are a lot of bands like that: taking their music out on the road, taking it directly to the people. It's gratifying that more than 35 years later, here I am and so many bands that were supposed to be "the next big thing" when we were coming out are gone. I've seen all the flavors come and go.

It gives you some hope for humanity that the cream usually rises to the top, that things that are honest and true tend to endure over things that are manufactured. Is that what you're saying?

Well, not always, but most of the time. At least, I hope.

There was a 10-year-old kid in front of me at the Danzig show, just freaking out and screaming along to the songs. Is that something you've come to expect—that one generation passes their fandom down to the next?

It's great when people bring their kids to the shows or kids discover your stuff. I liken it to when I was a kid and was discovering bands that weren't of my generation and I would go to the show. Sometimes I talk to fans at the end of the shows and kids will tell me it's their first rock concert and I'm always like, "Really? Where you been?" And they'll say stuff like, "Well, I used to go to raves a lot" or "I listen to a lot of stuff on my computer." And I'm like, "Good. Get out of the house. Go experience life and the world. Life and the world is not just on your computer. That's just someone else telling you about what's going on out there. You should go out there yourself and experience life. Go to shows. Go have lunch at a restaurant. See other humans. Talk to them. Get out there."

I think sometimes that's frightening to some people in our post-digital age. Connecting can be scary. I think a sign of that and something that is a huge pet peeve of mine is when you go to see a show and there are a million glowing iPhones in the air. I feel like people use their phones to somehow block them, emotionally, from what is happening at a concert. It's difficult for people to have the courage to be engaged and present. How do you feel about something like iPhones coming out in droves at shows?

Well, you are always going to have some people act like idiots at shows. But I think the reason why it doesn't happen so much at our shows is that they're there for the *experience*...for what I'm trying to give them. If you come and see us, you're not coming to see the record be played live exactly how it sounds recorded. You're coming to experience this crazy energy that's coming off the stage and you get it and you send it back to me and I'll send it back out to you, 20 times as powerful. I'm trying to make some kind of experience for you. It's not just a concert. In fact, it should be some kind of ritual: you should lose your fucking mind for those two hours we're on stage. You should go out of your fucking mind! That's really what I'm trying to do. The sing-along? That goes back to

PHOTO COURTESY OF JEANEEN LUND

early punk rock. It's about everyone being a part of it. You know the words? Then fucking sing along with me. You wanna scream your head off? Do it! And you can hear it. When we do "Mother", for instance, I don't even have to encourage them—I just hold the mic up and they sing along. It's pretty cool. I am very lucky because people connect with what I'm trying to say and the music means something to them. That's really what music is about.

What were some of those first moments of catharsis for you at a live show? Of going to a concert and losing your shit?

The first live band I saw as a kid was Black Sabbath. And I remember there being things I liked about them and things I didn't like about them. I like singers who go crazy on stage, like James Brown. And I don't like singers that just stand there. So that's what I realized: when I saw Black Sabbath, the most exciting person to watch in the band was Geezer Butler because he was going crazy. Tony Iommi was standing in the center where a singer would normally be, and Ozzy was off to the side, clapping his hands. I just remember that even though I liked the

music, as a live performance, I probably connected more with Elvis or an Iggy Pop as far as vocalists go. I liked people that walked around and engaged the audience and talked to them. In that respect, I like Elvis and someone like Iggy who were communicating and going to the audience and saying, "This is me, here I am—who are you?" Elvis would do his thing, go down into the audience and interact. Iggy took it even further, and actually dove out into the audience and cut that line—he crossed it. I actually just did an intro to an Iggy book where I said that Iggy was probably the first rock singer to truly erase the line between the performer and the fans. I don't think anyone ever dove into the audience before Iggy.

There is a freedom inherent in what he does and what you do on stage. There is never a shtick. There is never this feeling of the performer being self-conscious or stagey. Your live shows are really raw. Is that what you hope the audience comes away feeling?

There are so many bands now that when they play their set, a lot of it is pre-recorded, *(CONTINUED ON PAGE 70)*

68

JOHN DARNIELLE

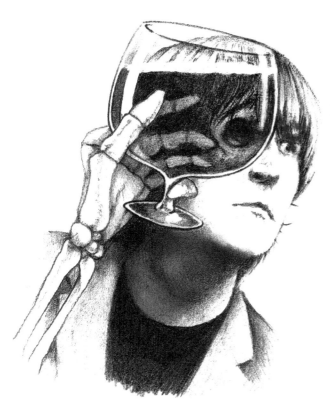

Re-purposed from a regular feature from our web site, Situation Critical presents artists with various life situations—some joyous, some terrible, some bizarre—to find out which songs, albums, or bands they would turn to under those specific circumstances. Earlier in 2013 we spoke with the Mountain Goats' John Darnielle, whose 2002 album All Hail West Texas *was recently named Best New Reissue.*

You're lifting weights at the gym...

There was a time in the late 1980s when I signed up for a gym even though I was very scrawny and a heavy smoker and not in good shape in any way. It was this giant muscle-dude gym, which was awesome, because if you can't bench anything and you work out at that gym, those dudes treat you like you are one of them. They'll come up and spot your miserable 80-pound press and sit there going, "It's all you! One more, man, one more!" But I specifically remember that was the first place I heard "Her Black Wings" by Danzig, and it was so perfect—this big doomy thing to be pumping iron to.

You're settling down for some light reading...

I'd go with the first song from the third Danzig record, "Godless", for contrast. Light reading; blackest of the black, darker than night, come to me my bleeding light.

You find a $20 bill on the sidewalk...

Lean down, light the $20 bill on fire, play Danzig's "Into the Mouth of Abandonment".

You're DJing your best friend's wedding...

This question presupposes that I have friends, which is kind of an unsafe presupposition, but OK—assuming I've got friends and they invite me to their wedding and ask me to DJ, what do I play for them? I thought long and hard about this, because weddings are really special, and the best song to play would be "How the Gods Kill" by Danzig.

You're waiting for the results of an important medical test...

This happens to me all the time, since I have a lot of medical testing done, so I know that I would listen to "Am I Demon" by Danzig.

You're home sick with the flu...

"Do You Wear the Mark" by Danzig.

You're throwing a dinner party...

Oak-hewn plates, Waterford crystal, and "See All You Were" by Danzig.

You're working a shitty data entry job that allows you to wear headphones...

"Twist of Cain", also by Danzig.

You just got home on Friday night and you're super drunk...

I know a lot of people would go with the Butterfield Blues Band, but I'm gonna have to say Danzig's "Pain in the World".

You're playing your child music for the first time...

There can only be the one answer.

(CONTINUED FROM PAGE 68) a computer running everything. And they get up there and do a puppet show or karaoke or something. I don't know what it is. I don't care about it. We don't do that.

You say you hate the internet. But you must use it to connect with your fans.

Sure. I mean, of course I use the internet. I have the Danzig and Verotik site and we post news there. The internet isn't all bad. It's like anything: it just gets abused. It's a good way to disseminate information, and also a good way to disseminate disinformation. You can put out stuff that is blatantly untrue and present it as fact on the internet. Governments around the world have been conducting disinformation campaigns for centuries. But now, with the internet, anyone can do it. Before you had to run a newspaper or a TV channel. But now, anyone can perpetrate untruths. Someone can go on there and say, for instance, "Pitchfork is out of business." And you're going to have to spend the week telling everyone that you're NOT out of business. The internet has no culpability. Anyone can get on there and just lie.

Sure. But at the same time, what about all those kids living in Nowhereville feeling isolated? What about the internet allowing them access to all sorts of knowledge and to your music, to things that they can connect with and ultimately love? Things that make them feel like they belong in some way? The internet is good for that, don't you think?

Yeah, but you know what? People always find this stuff. That's what we did. We didn't have the internet and we found good music, movies, comics, etc. We heard about bands from this area or that area and we went and saw them play. We became their friends. There was an underground of information. And we were able to find out about things that we ended up loving. I don't know how that exists now. The underground doesn't exist any more.

Well, the underground lasts for about a minute before it's overground.

Exactly. I just still do it the same way I always did it: I design the album covers, I write the songs, and then I take them to everybody.

Is there anything you haven't done yet that you'd like to do?

Yes. I want to put my mark on film. That's what I've been concentrating on the past few years—taking a lot of the ideas I've created and translating them to film. I think once that's done, there will be a great weight lifted off my shoulders.

That seems like a logical next step for someone who already is so involved in creating comics, art, music.

Well, you know, I went to the New York Institute of Photography in the 1970s, and I studied film, photography, and art. Film is really important to me, and it was a big part of working with Rick Rubin in the beginning of Danzig, because it was really important to him as well. We also liked a lot of the same directors, and this led to me directing a lot of Danzig's music videos—that was really important to me as part of learning about that aspect of film. So the next step really is to direct a couple of feature films—some based on my comics, some live action. I've got a lot of ideas and we'll have to see which one moves first.

Let's get back to what we were talking about at the beginning, about the range of ages at your show. What do you think keeps bringing new generations of kids to your music? What is it they're responding to?

It could be so many different things. Maybe they like the music. Maybe they like the vocals. It could be they just like the realness of it. I don't know. I'm just lucky people like it. And I try to be true to myself. And in being true to myself, I know I'm being true to the people that have followed me all these years and to the new fans as well. And if I've learned anything over the last four decades, it is that the best way to be true to your audience is to be true to yourself.

Jessica Hundley is a writer and filmmaker. She writes for a bunch of mags, pens books about people like Gram Parsons and Dennis Hopper, makes documentaries on subjects like the heavy rock underground and Latino Morrissey fans, and directs music videos for artists ranging from folk legend Linda Perhacs to scuzz rockers Zig Zags. You can check out more of her work at jessicahundley.com.

KURT VILE

&

WATERY LOVE

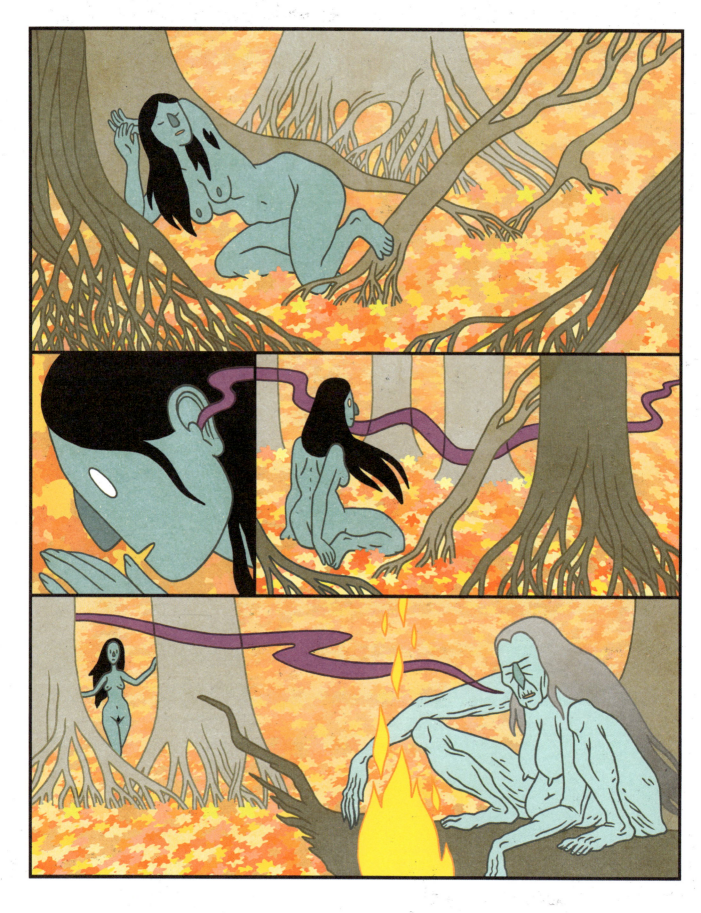

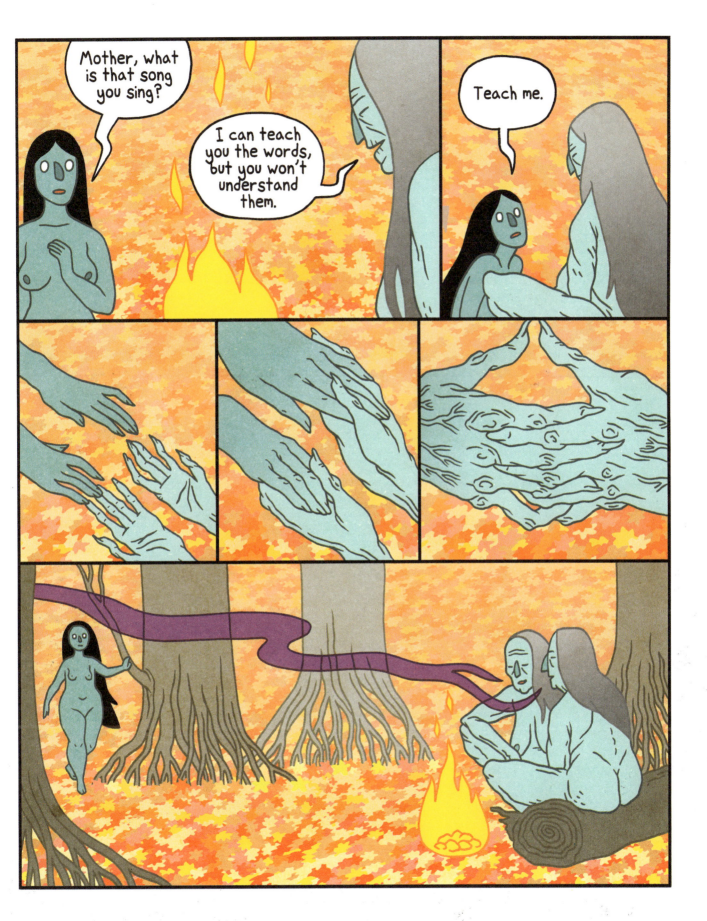

Jukebox Elegy

BY MIMI LIPSON

"... an iPod can never be a jukebox, because it reflects a single consciousness. It leaves no room for serendipity."

I prefer the old ones, the kind that play 45s, though they are becoming rare. I liked it when they took quarters. You could listen to the coin drop and the gear-turning mechanism engage. It always seemed crazy to me that there was a turntable hidden within those mysterious flanks, like something from a Max Fleischer cartoon. Maybe it's a leftover childhood impulse that makes me yearn to put a coin in a slot and get something back, however ephemeral or dubious in value: a rock-hard gumball; a small handful of stale nuts; a penny, squashed flat and stamped with the Statue of Liberty. "Superfreak", "Delta Dawn", "Okie From Muskogee".

Ideally, it is early evening. The room is practically empty—just a few leftover daytime drinkers, watching out of the corners of their eyes as you lean over the glass and run your finger across the rows and down the columns of labels, printed on pale pink and blue and green paper: two songs to a slip, with the artist's name in the center band. There are only a hundred songs to choose from, but that is as it should be. A limited selection takes the pressure off. The song does not have to be great; it just has to be good enough for that moment, in that company, in that place. After all, you aren't choosing an epitaph or a yearbook motto. It is just three minutes of your life.

Of course a song, unlike a gumball, is something you share with everyone who happens to be in the bar. It can be an icebreaker for the shyest among us—especially useful in unfamiliar territory.

These days the music in your corner bar, especially if it caters to a hip young crowd, is likely coming from your bartender's iPod. With the shuffle setting turned on, it superficially resembles a jukebox. Your bartender might even be playing Barbara Lynn and Jimmy Smith—all the songs you would have picked out on a well-stocked jukebox. But it won't be the same, because an iPod is a monologue and a jukebox is a conversation anyone can join.

The invention of the jukebox is credited to Louis T. Glass, who presented the first "nickel-in-the-slot phonograph" to the world in 1889. For our purposes, though, Glass's machine wasn't really a jukebox. It only accommodated one wax cylinder at a time, and you had to listen with earphones that looked like a stethoscope. The machine's social aspects came into play in the 1920s, first becoming popular in the juke joints of the rural South from which they took their name. "Juke" is a term of possible Gullah origin meaning "dance" or "fuck" or, more likely, both. Later, manufacturers would try to distance themselves from the association by promoting the use of clinical-sounding alternatives like "record machine," but the term "jukebox" stuck.

Unlike radio, the jukebox was a racially integrated medium from the get-go—a telegram that passed through segregated Southern rooms, where hillbilly records first rubbed shoulders with delta blues. Without jukeboxes, there would be no rock 'n' roll. During the Great Depression they went mainstream, popping up in coffee shops and roadside diners across the country as inexpensive entertainment for people who could not afford to see a live orchestra and who might not even have a radio set at home. Production slowed during World War II, when the Big Three—Wurlitzer, Seeburg, and Rock-Ola—retooled for munitions, but it surged again when the troops began to return. In 1946, Wurlitzer rolled out its most popular model, the 1015, considered by aficionados to be the platonic ideal of jukebox styling, at once gaudy and deluxe, with bubble tubes and lava lamp colors all housed in a rich walnut veneer cabinet.

For me the Wurlitzer 1015 is also the platonic ideal

TOPS – PHILADELPHIA, PA

of cornball nostalgia. It puts me in mind of that hateful word, "retro." The genuine article fades seamlessly into the ersatz: turtle-waxed tailfins, Johnny Rockets, and Bob Seger singing "Still Like That Old-Time Rock and Roll" (incidentally, the #3 all-time jukebox hit single). I remember the moment it first occurred to me that someone I considered my contemporary was over the hill. He showed me a jukebox he had just bought. It probably wasn't a Wurlitzer 1015, but that's how I picture it. It is possible his jukebox was a replica; as I said, it doesn't matter. Either way, it embarrassed me terribly. This person was in his early 20s and he was already amassing "collectibles" like a middle-aged insurance salesman.

Perhaps it's unfair that I held this particular jukebox in contempt because of its over-the-top styling. It was, after all, the styling that he wanted. This was the mid-1980s, and the world was still full of jukeboxes. They were in pizza parlors and bowling alleys and bus station bars: squat, utilitarian things with scratched glass, covered in graffiti. My friend would no more have brought one of those things home than he would have installed a parking meter in his driveway. Really, the problem with buying a jukebox and setting it up in his living room was that he had missed the whole *point* of a jukebox. It is not home decor; it's supposed to exist out in the world some-

where, fulfilling its role as a device for anchoring music in time and space.

I will never again, for instance, hear Alice Cooper's "I'm Eighteen" or "Sky Pilot" by The Animals without thinking fondly of Tops, a second-story pool bar presided over by a Fishtown native named Ruthie—a bartender of the tough-but-fair school who did not suffer fools gladly. I discovered Tops soon after I moved to Philadelphia for graduate school. Sometimes, when I was feeling lonely, I would climb the steep staircase from 15th Street and turn the tight corner past the bathrooms. Wedged into the narrow hallway was a nondescript jukebox. Let's say it was a 1985 Rock-Ola SuperSound 2. I would put in a dollar and play my two songs before sitting at the bar and saying hi to Ruthie. Why "I'm Eighteen" and "Sky Pilot"? I do not want either of them playing at my funeral, but they are good songs.

I began to date a postdoc named Robert, an affable pothead from the Bay Area whose musical tastes I didn't share. He liked Camper Van Beethoven. The jukebox at Tops didn't have any of their songs, but it did have "Eurotrash Girl" by Cracker, which I would play for Robert when we went there together. And so, though it's a song neither he nor I had any strong feeling for, in my mind it became "our song." When I hear it (which hasn't hap-

HOTSY TOTSY CLUB – BAY AREA, CA

pened in years), I think all at once of the wobbly tables and indoor-outdoor carpeting in the little corral off to one side of the pool table, and of Robert, the astrophysicist with the surfer-blond hair.

Around the time I was haunting Tops, machines that played 45s were giving way to machines that played CDs, and in the last few years those have largely been replaced by internet jukeboxes. In less than 20 years, we have gone from a hundred songs to a thousand songs to machines with 40 gigabyte drives that hold up to 10,000 songs and are connected to remote databases that offer infinite choices. Choosing something to play requires scrolling through the alphabet. You pretty much have to know what you are looking for or you will be browsing all night. It is hard to find someone who actually likes internet jukeboxes. Because the selection is essentially identical from one bar to the next, the general consensus is that they make every place more like every other place.

No technology dies without a funeral, and these days fetishization is never far behind. Refurbished jukeboxes are finding their way into places like the Hotsy Totsy Club, a bar in the East Bay that features *Mad Men*-style cocktails and a Modess tampon dispenser in the ladies' room. The owner, Michael Valladares, described his bar to the Oakland North website as "a historical recreation,"

the centerpiece of which is a 1967 Wurlitzer Americana stocked with discs from his personal collection. The selections sound great: Desmond Dekker, James Brown, Herb Alpert and his Tijuana Brass. I would love to relax with a Negroni and listen to "The Lonely Bull". There is nothing wrong with having a cool-looking gadget that plays excellent music, and maybe it makes no difference to the patrons, but they're still missing out on the jukebox experience.

The word I am straining to avoid is authenticity. There is no faking the patina that accumulates in a bar over the years—the accretion of beer spills, dirty palms, duct tape on vinyl, fixtures that break and can't be exactly matched. If the Hotsy Totsy Club sticks around long enough, it will become authentic in its own right. I have less hope for Valladares' jukebox, which is essentially a beautiful iPod, and an iPod can never be a jukebox, because it reflects a single consciousness. It leaves no room for serendipity.

Even when they were ubiquitous, I don't think those old jukeboxes created a sense of place in the way people imagine, with biker songs in a biker bar and cowboy songs in a cowboy bar. For the most part, they were a hodgepodge of recent Top 40 hits, golden oldies, forgotten Christmas songs, novelty records that could earn the

HOP LOUIE'S – LOS ANGELES, CA

enmity of your fellow drinkers or even get you 86'd by the bartender, and sometimes a stray Big Band number. The musical selection might lean this way or that depending on the clientele, but sometimes oddly inappropriate songs were buried in the mix like booby traps waiting to be sprung—Sergeant Barry Sadler at a soul bar, or the Mary Jane Girls at a backwoods roadhouse. And there were quirks that only the regulars knew. You might, for instance, hit 22A expecting "Little Red Corvette" and instead have to hang your head in shame through "Hip to Be Square" by Huey Lewis and the News.

It's the anomalies that stick in your mind. When I think of Hop Louie's, for example—a pagoda-shaped bar in the Chinatown mall in Los Angeles—I hear "In the Mood" performed by the Glenn Miller Orchestra. At the Drinking Fountain, a taproom in Boston where I used to shoot pool, it was Elvis hiccupping soulfully through "Blue Christmas" in high summer while I stood in the gust of an industrial floor fan and chalked my sweaty hands. Or else it was Connie Francis. I vividly remember watching a group of older women from the neighborhood play "Stupid Cupid" over and over, jumping up and down so hard I thought their white Russians would fall off the table.

Of course, an accurate log of what played on the juke-

box while I was shooting pool at the Drinking Fountain would probably turn out to be pretty uninteresting. The bulk of it, I am sure, was U2, Hank Williams, Jr., Guns N' Roses, Mariah Carey—a tour of the commercial radio of the day, more or less. This in and of itself suggests continuity with the past. The jukeboxes I knew at the Drinking Fountain or Tops were not so different from their siblings, the cigarette machine and the pay phone: bar furniture, sitting in their corners accumulating dust and band stickers until it was time to serve their purpose. At one time, though, jukeboxes played an important role in the music industry as a first stop for debuting new records. They even had their own category in the Billboard charts. Inventory was kept up by vendors with close ties to the record industry and, often, the mob. For me, a slight whiff of crime lingers around any jukebox old enough to play records: payola and slot machines, the back room, the underworld.

I am not sure when all that stopped. It was probably a gradual change. I only know that the gap between jukeboxes and the Billboard charts had widened by the time I started going to bars, to the point that a song labeled "Hit" could be 5, 10, 15 years old. Vendors and record companies apparently moved on to ventures with higher profit margins. I think the typical hodgepodge I encoun-

DRINKING FOUNTAIN–BOSTON, MA

tered was, as much as anything, a product of neglect: records left behind after they slipped down the charts, seasonal stock that did not get rotated, occasional rogue disks smuggled in by the proprietor and identifiable by their handwritten labels—all of it collecting like dust bunnies as the roster of songs drifted ever farther from the charts. The selection was small enough that genuine browsing was possible, and anyone scanning the rows and columns could find the oddballs.

A lot has been said about the paradoxically narrowing effects of infinite choice. In the age of Google, everyone knows about confirmation bias, about the mental fog of aimless web surfing. But less is said about the joys of a limited selection. I have found that internet natives will nod along, up to the point where you suggest that you might be happier if that ocean of consumable culture dried up again. It is hard to sell the idea that people lived rich and fulfilling lives with a bookshelf, six channels, and two milk crates of LPs—that we were not hopelessly stunted by our constraints. In fact, the reverse was true. If I'd had Nickelodeon when I was growing up, or a VCR, would I have watched thousands of hours of TV intended for other people—"Victory at Sea", "Candlepins for Cash", "Flash Gordon", "I Claudius", "Car 54 Where Are You?", "The Magic of Oil Painting", "The French Chef with Julia

Child", or, for that matter, a single frame of the Watergate hearings? If I'd had to scroll alphabetically through all the TV shows that ever existed, would I have reached into an unpromising black and white past and discovered Eve Arden and Jack Benny and Ernie Kovacs?

It occurs to me that I am not making a very good case for jukeboxes. Maybe there isn't a case to be made. They were, and soon they will be no more, except in a few suburban rec rooms and some historically recreated bars. Their memory will live on in the titles of a hundred songs. "Jukebox Hero" by Foreigner, "Jukebox Mama" by Link Wray, "Wurlitzer Jukebox" by Young Marble Giants. We'll know them from *American Graffiti* and *Goodfellas* and *Who's Afraid of Virginia Woolf* and a thousand other films. And maybe in some bar somewhere, a bored young person will scroll through the "I's" and pick out "In the Mood", performed by the Glenn Miller Orchestra. I suppose anything is possible. ✍

Mimi Lipson lives in Kingston, New York. Her writing has appeared in the Harvard Review, BOMB, This Long Century, Joyland, *and other places. She has a short story collection coming out in April 2014 from Yeti Books.*

NABIL

in

PARIS

NABIL

in

PARIS

DRINKING FOUNTAIN—BOSTON, MA

N A B I L

i n

P A R I S

Documenting music events in 2013 is an act of both ubiquity and novelty. On one hand, almost everybody these days has a nice camera and a platform to showcase their photos, which guarantees any event of a decent size will be covered from every angle leaving almost nothing to the imagination. On the other hand, this presents the idea of professionally shooting a concert with the intention to document as almost pointless—unless you're entering the situation with a focused point of view and artistic objective. Capturing that perfect moment of bass face with the utmost clarity is fine, but looking beyond the stage show and being able to illustrate the experience and a narrative is something that requires a certain chutzpah and vision that eludes most photographers.

Born in Chicago, but then spending most of his young life in Australia, Nabil Elderkin got started in photography by shooting the surfing culture that surrounded him. When he moved back to Chicago in his late teens, he stuck with photography but turned his focus to music. He famously scored his first big project by buying kanyewest.com three weeks before Kanye signed to Roc-A-Fella. When they came asking for it, instead of trying to capitalize on the moment financially, Nabil asked to shoot Kanye instead. Not only would this serendipitous incident foreshadow future success (he's since gone on to shoot videos for Bon Iver, Frank Ocean, Arctic Monkeys, Antony and the Johnsons, James Blake, and more), it also shows a trait that's been indicative of his style ever since. He doesn't necessarily have an aesthetic signature; his work is always rooted in an idea first, letting style communicate the concept and feeling. In working with him a few times, I can attest that he'll sacrifice anything personally (he doesn't seem to sleep much) in order to execute to his standards.

In 2011, we hosted our first music festival in Paris and invited Nabil to come and shoot the event. What we got back wasn't just a shot-by-shot roundup of each band, it was a look into one artist's weekend at Paris' Grande Halle de la Villette. We present these photos for the first time in this inaugural issue of *The Pitchfork Review.* MICHAEL RENAUD

1

2

3

4

6

7

9

10

11

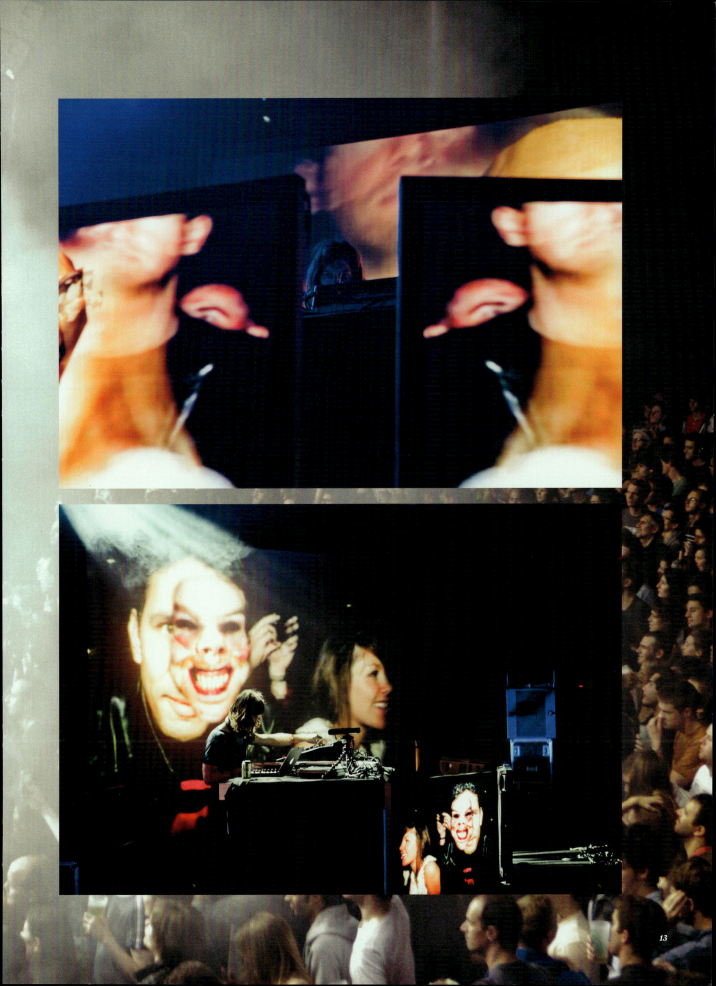

16

17

23

24

Control P

ILLUSTRATION BY TIM LAHAN

NO HEROES

Savages want to focus our fleeting attention—with guitars, drums, and fury. Turn away at your own risk.

By Laura Snapes

ILLUSTRATION BY MICHAEL DEFORGE

"I'm trying to talk to people about themselves, to just tell the truth, and maybe that's why people come to see us, as an inspiration for emancipation."

—JEHNNY BETH

114

In February 2013, Savages played a show at David Lynch's exclusive Paris nightclub, Silencio. As the red velvet curtains opened—of course there were curtains—the four-piece peered out into a room of perched and propped Lynchian devotees swirling $20 cocktails. The band stared at them silently for 30 confrontational seconds before drummer Fay Milton broke the war of attrition.

The following night, the group walked on stage at London's Electric Ballroom for their biggest hometown show yet. Once again, the music didn't start immediately. This time, though, it was not intentional. The dude manning the monitors, who had been uncooperative and snide during soundcheck, had vanished. He did not reappear. Three awkward minutes passed.[1] Finally, frontwoman Jehnny Beth flashed her gimlet eye and seethed, "I think we're all fucking ready, right? This is called 'Shut Up'." Ayse Hassan's bass and Gemma Thompson's guitar rumbled in, restlessly steering the

---

[1] "Do you have to fuck off or can we do 'Fuckers'?" Jehnny Beth asked at the end of soundcheck. "You can fuck off, it's a shit song anyway," came the reply—it was hard to interpret what level of familiarity the male voice had with the band, whether it was a joke or an insult. The next day, Jehnny wrote to the promoter, asking, "Did someone smash his brain out after the show?"

PHOTO BY SE YOUNG AU

Jehnny Beth

sound. Beth, a heart-faced woman with a severe Mia Farrow crop, jogged on the spot, circling her fists as if poised to sprint, or planning a sharp right hook.

In the café of an artsy east London cinema the next afternoon, the mood was good-humored, though the shrill coffee machine aggravated their severe hangovers. Milton went to bed at 7 am after being dragged to a gay club when the band got kicked out of their own after-party, where they hung out with the DJ and played Bowie records. A week-old bruise on her left eyelid showed when she rolled her eyes while the band discussed the previous night's sound issues. They were certain the venue's monitor tech didn't like being told what to do by women. When Savages started performing in early 2012, a number of similar experiences persuaded them to employ their own sound team.

"One guy gave us really awful sound, then came and apologized afterward, saying, 'Sorry, I didn't realize you were going to be good,'" said Milton. "'*I didn't realize you could play like that*,'" mocked Thompson, a trilobite tattoo visible on her forearm as she ruffled her ostensibly home-cut hair.

"People tell me, 'Don't let the fuckers get you down,'" Beth said, raising her eyebrows. That mantra formed the chorus to the castigating "Fuckers", last night's abrasive set closer, where she gnashed at the edict like Nick Cave with barbed wire for teeth. "I'm like, '*No*. Don't let the fuckers get you down...and *then* give them a lesson!'"[2]

In the 18 months since Savages formed—three friends, plus a brutal drummer unearthed via recommendations—they've executed their mu-

sic, shows, and business with ruthless efficiency. In one of their declarative mission statements, which appear online and are appended to their releases, they call the band a "self-affirming voice to help experience our girlfriends, our husbands, our jobs, our erotic life, and the place music occupies in our lives differently."

Their music borrows from post-punk's dynamics, hardcore's uncompromising abrasion, and the overdrive of metal, with songs rewritten until they're reduced to the most essential ideas. At the heart of the uncompromising quartet is a vitriolic refusal of victimization, though they shrug off potential affiliations with riot grrrl and the dogmatic approach of a band like Fugazi. Instead, strident lyrics about embracing creative and erotic pleasures eschew soapboxing in favor of something more instinctive.

Considering all that, *Silence Yourself* might seem like a strangely bossy title for the debut album of a band so concerned with self-expression. But it's more about shedding distractions. "We're submerged by voices, opinions, images," said Beth. "They take us away from who we are. The idea with Savages is to get back to this more focused attention, so you're harder to reach."

As a child, Jehnny Beth's theater director parents wouldn't let her watch television or do "kid things." Born Camille Berthomier in Poitiers, a small city in western France, on December 24, 1984, one of her earliest memories is of touring Russia with one of her father's plays. She loved the films her parents showed her by Hitchcock, Truffaut, and John Cassavetes, whose New Wave sensibilities played well in France. *Silence Yourself* begins with a sample of dialogue from Cassavetes' 1977 drama *Opening Night,* which deals with an older actress's struggle to pursue

---

[2] "What I liked about the song was that you could say such a potentially happy message but in such an angry way," says Jehnny of "Fuckers". "I suddenly realized that I couldn't pretend that I don't let the fuckers get me down, because it's not true, I would pretend I am someone I am not. I would pretend I'm a super human, and me, I've found a solution of not being put down by fuckers, which is not true! I just sing it until maybe one day I hope I will not feel this anger. I always think there's a line in that song that always makes me think of the Smiths song. When I say, 'You can fight until you're dead, they put the books upon your head, you can drive away from town, don't let the fuckers get you down,' and 'you can drive away from town,' for me, it's like 'There is a Light That Never Goes Out'."

"People tell me they think pornography is bad for women and assume I'm going to understand, but I watch a lot of pornography. It's been very important for me, to liberate myself from the pressure of romanticism and the myth of a woman's pleasure."

—JEHNNY BETH

her career in accordance with her beliefs. "She doesn't want to follow the rules, so she's fighting, and that's what I like about the film," explained Beth. "She would never give up."

Beth's parents "emancipated themselves" from their agricultural backgrounds by reading and going to university, and were keen to impress the importance of academic study on Jehnny and her sister. "They were very open intellectually, although still coming from a Catholic background—an interesting mix!" she said with a yelp.

On a cold afternoon in January, Beth was the last member to present herself for an individual grilling at a central London café decorated like a mad aunt's parlor. The band had insisted on being interviewed separately, in consecutive half-hour sessions, a turn of events made no less odd by the fact that Beth documented our conversation on an enormous tape recorder that looked like it was stolen from a Cold War museum. "For my memories," she said.[3]

She repeatedly returned to the word "emancipation." When she was in her late teens, she met Nicolas Congé, aka Johnny Hostile, who she called "a big part in my emancipation as a person, but also as a musician." They remain together, having moved to London in late 2006, adopting new names to form John and Jehn, a Kills-like duo. The band took precedence over Beth's burgeoning acting career. She starred in 2005's *À travers la forêt* and 2009's *Sodium Babies*, two French-made fantasy/horror films. In old interviews, Hostile joked that he kidnapped her.

"Both of us wanted to avoid boredom in a small town in France," Hostile told me. "We became hyperactive in all aspects of life: how we deal with our job, our sex life, our families, our friends. She emancipated me equally."

"They moved around in a very menacing, jerky fashion," remembers British Sea Power frontman

---

[3] My meetings with Savages for this piece frequently made me feel as though I was the one under observation, that they were trying to psych me out to some extent—at first only meeting them in pairs and then individually, watching them confer in whispers as the groups changed over, and only receiving the band as a whole on the third round of interviewing. On that day, at the Rich Mix cinema café in east London, the first remark on my tape is me asking Jehnny Beth where her tape recorder was. The other women looked surprised. "I was looking for, I dunno, we were looking for samples for the album, things like that, I wanted to see if something would come out," she said. I didn't believe her for a second.

Savages

Scott "Yan" Wilkinson, who often had John and Jehn open for his band and gave Savages their first gig in January 2012. "You couldn't tell if they were going to have a kiss or a fight—made me think of erotic roosters."

Hostile is always around Savages, his swooping black coat and crooked, Gallic good looks providing an impressive presence wherever he goes. Although he co-produced their album, his role seems to challenge rather than control; none of the other three members visibly resent his suggestions. He is aware, though, that he can be domineering. Savages was Thompson's baby, and when she originally asked Hostile to front the band, he declined. "I respect her too much," he said. "I didn't want to waste her time with me trying to change everything. She deserved someone easier to work with."

Beth said Hostile's role in her liberation meant she couldn't call herself a feminist. Although she agrees with the movement's aims for equality, she has misgivings about its wider motivations and is fascinated when women put a feminist reading on Savages. "They tell me they think pornography is bad for women and assume I'm going to understand," she said. "The thing is, I watch a lot of pornography. It's been very important for me, to liberate myself from the pressure of romanticism, the myth of a woman's pleasure."[4]

Toward the end of *Silence Yourself* is a song called "Hit Me" that was recorded entirely live, which makes its Meat Puppets-playing-axel-grinders maelstrom even more striking. "I took a beating today/ And that was the best I ever had," Beth moans, adopting the perspective of her favorite porn star, Belladonna, who gained widespread notoriety following a 2003 interview with Diane Sawyer in which she cried about some of her experiences, and was subsequently used

as a straw man for porn's "manipulative evils" by lobbyists. (She spoke out afterward about how the editors of *Primetime* misrepresented her as a victim.)

Elsewhere on the record, Beth sings about dark sexual liberation, unmasking one's soul, vanquishing faceless cowards—and finding yourself sleeping with them, too. The album's most surprising lyric is also its most domestic. "How come I've been doing things with you/ I would never tell my mum?" Beth sings on the swaggering, Suede-worthy "Strife". She describes the song as being about "almost showing your weakness" and "that sense of becoming a child again, when you're doing these crazy, dirty things."

Savages' honesty about the complexities of female sexuality places them in an under-populated but fervent lineage that stretches from Patti Smith through Liz Phair, PJ Harvey, the Yeah Yeah Yeahs, and beyond. (At her most aggressive, Beth's wail is a dead ringer for Karen O's pixelated yowl.) For these women, the desire for violent or so-called deviant sexual pleasure is empowering and not simply a cheap signifier of "transgression" or vulnerability.

"I'm trying to talk to people about themselves, to say things as they are, to just tell the truth," expressed Beth. "And maybe that's why people come to see us, as an inspiration for emancipation." She referred to a trans woman in the process of gender reassignment surgery who recently wrote to the band. "Savages was helping her go through this process, the pain," she said. "We were all really moved by it."

In November 2012, Savages entered the Fish Factory studio in northwest London to begin recording their debut album. They spent three hermetic weeks there with Hostile and co-pro-

---

[4] The band seem disdainful of feminism beyond its basic aims of equality; when I met Gemma Thompson and Ayse Hassan for their joint interview in Bristol in December, Gemma said that she perceived the word "as asking for help, pitying in a way. To all of us, feminism is looking from below. It's kind of about saying, 'We're stronger than that. We've passed that.' It gets to a point where you have to take more action, and I think with the lyrics and the performance, it is about that, about the action and performance rather than saying why, or what it means."

ducer Rodaidh McDonald, who worked on both xx albums, How to Dress Well's *Total Loss*, and heaps of others. The first Savages single was essentially recorded in a tricked-out cupboard in Beth and Hostile's north London house, where each part was recorded separately. McDonald proposed the opposite approach for the album, setting them up like the live band they are.

Silence Yourself comprises 11 songs that shriek and writhe within a consistently ominous ambience. It's exhilaratingly aggressive. The guitar work on "I Am Here" takes cues from post-hardcore titans Converge, while the cymbals on "She Will" borrow from krautrock greats Faust. The groan that opens "Husbands" is sampled from a film Thompson found while working at London's Natural History Museum that captures the sound of lava solidifying underwater.

Although the band laughs guiltily at how picky they were in the studio, McDonald appreciated it. "It's unusual to work with a guitar band where each member is deeply into experimenting within their role, and pushing it to the extreme," he said. "It's refreshing."

Only the final song of each side, "Dead Nature" and closer "Marshall Dear", are more subdued—the latter features piano by Beth, who is a trained jazz pianist, and would feel at home playing in a sleazy smoker's den. The song leaves the album enticingly open-ended.

Still, there is no ignoring their obvious influences. Savages recall a number of post-punk, no wave, and metal bands. "I call it the 'Old Man's Disease,' which I had when I was 21," says BBC 6Music DJ Marc Riley, debating whether the band's originality, or potential lack thereof, matters. Riley was an early member of The Fall and significant enough in the band's career that Mark E. Smith later directed at least three overt cuss

songs aimed at him. Riley gave Savages their first live radio session back in May 2012. "I remember the first time I heard the Jesus and Mary Chain, I thought, 'I've got *White Light / White Heat*, why bother?' But of course you're wrong to think like that. Savages get compared to Public Image Ltd and Siouxsie and the Banshees, but the songs are great. That's all that matters."

Savages have found another fervent admirer in Portishead founder Geoff Barrow, whose crush began when they played his hometown, Bristol, last August. They met, and did some non-committal recording later in the summer—just friends, experimenting, and no, you can't hear it.

I met Barrow in Bristol on another bitterly cold night in mid-December 2012, at a dank pub on an out-of-town road where it was impossible to buy cigarettes, but very easy to get a "special" massage at the Village Sauna. "This is a band like My Bloody Valentine," Barrow said over a beer, smoothing his Earth t-shirt. "One of those classic bands that you just *love*. They're proper." Next door at the Exchange, preparations were afoot for Apocatastasis, a Christmas party thrown by Barrow's Invada Records, where Savages would play their last date of 2012.

One of Barrow's other bands, Beak>, opened Savages' Electric Ballroom date, and Savages returned the favor by playing before Portishead on their European tour in the summer of 2013. The mutual admiration is strong. It has to be, as Savages make clear that they aren't wild about opening for *anyone*. Talking about their experience as a supporting act for guitar rocking also-rans the Vaccines last May, Beth jutted her jaw. "It was shit," she spat unexpectedly. Although Savages' then-managers didn't force them into it, it seems to have been at their suggestion. They also wanted the band to sign with a label—any label—by June 2012, a notion Beth balked at. (John and Jehn remain in a bind over a previous bad deal.) "It was a bad time for us," she said. "We almost lost the band."

On May 29, 2013, Savages released their debut single, "Flying to Berlin" b/w "Husbands", and headed to Salford the following day to play their 6Music session for Marc Riley. It was a pivotal day. "There was so much tension in the air," Milton said. "We worried that we were going to fuck up live on the radio." They didn't. "The session was amazing," said Riley.

In the van on the way back to London the next day, they decided to sack their managers. Thompson and Beth severed ties in person. "It was a *good fucking thing to do*," Beth said, with no small amount of intensity.

In the end, Savages refused to sign to a label until they had finished making their album, which they say they paid for themselves. It's all about rejecting what they see as a severely outdated industry and generational hierarchies. In short, they don't take advice easily, though their new manager, John Best, was a Britpop mastermind.

"Even supposedly experienced people don't know how to do things now because everything is broken down," Beth said. "When people tell you you have to support another band for some reason—that doesn't really make sense any more! Our generation doesn't believe in elites. The filmmaker Adam Curtis said we are an apocalyptic generation. I thought that was great—that's exactly where our name comes from."

Over our three meetings, the singer regularly talked of her admiration for Michael Gira, and how he chose to end Swans in the late 1990s rather than jeopardize his vision. "Some people's souls are too big and strong to do the compromis-

es constantly asked of you when you play rock music, because it's not considered an art," she said of him.

Though Beth and Hostile run their own small imprint, *Silence Yourself* was released through Matador Records. Over email, Beth explained that she doesn't think the deal merits congratulations. "I have no pride or happiness left in me for these kind of things," she wrote. "I came to a point where I absolutely had to demystify the cult surrounding indie labels. I see things differently, I guess. I believe artists make their own success. No record labels are my heroes today."

Although she is the most vocal member of the band, Beth was in fact the last to join Savages. After Hostile turned down Thompson's offer to front the band, Beth sent a tentative email asking if she could try out, to Thompson's total, delighted surprise. "From the first rehearsal, it was very productive. We weren't just there to tell each other we were great," Milton said when she arrived for her one-on-one interview, carrying a copy of *The Fountainhead*.

Hassan was Thompson's original foil: they met through the bassist's crazy Halloween parties and went on to play in the band Hindley. "It was a kind of My Bloody Valentine noise-fest," Thompson recalled. "We played at every shit-hole in London. We had our own smoke machine, lights, costumes. No matter where we were, it was about perfecting the performance." Her meticulous presentational streak remains. Savages no longer play "shit-holes" with any desperate regularity, but they curate everything from posters to video trailers, support slots, visuals, and the music between acts. Their show at the Electric Ballroom was a comprehensive display of how maintaining such total control can result in something truly uncompromising.

∗
~

"I absolutely had to demystify the cult surrounding indie labels. I believe artists make their own success. No record labels are my heroes today."

—JEHNNY BETH

Laura Snapes *is the Features Editor for* NME. *She's a former Associate Editor at Pitchfork and her writing has also been featured in* The Guardian, The Observer, Uncut, The Stool Pigeon, Under the Radar, *and at* The Quietus *and* eMusic.

From the start, a creaking chime—like midnight sounding over the River Styx—played over the venue's sound system, though no one really noticed. Attentions were piqued, however, when a woman in white suddenly got on her back near the bar end of the room. Knees bent, she used her feet to push herself down toward the stage, narrowly avoiding getting stepped on. Another four dancers followed, a space clearing around them. They reached the end of the room and rolled onto their fronts, crawling in a circle at a deathly slow pace, as if the air had the consistency of wet cement. Eventually they rose together, heads bowed, shoulders locked, looking like decapitated corpses. The spectacle was intimidating, tedious, and awe-inspiring. It went on for 35 minutes, making some of the crowd hilariously antsy. "I don't think they're about to do the 'Thriller' dance, do you?" an incessantly chattering woman asked her friends.

Milton's friend, Fernanda Muñoz-Newsome, had choreographed the piece, titled "Rewind-It". Her motivation was to create "something that would not be easy to sit back and watch." Smoking in the freezing back alley, Thompson explained that the impetus to stage the piece came from a performance by Wire at the same venue 33 years prior, captured on 1981's *Document & Eyewitness*. Wire antagonized the audience by scrapping the hits and including a bizarre Dadaist cabaret that constantly interrupted their set. The skinhead-heavy crowd bottled them.

"The concept was to challenge the audience," she said, shivering in a long black coat. It certainly showed gall to subject a Thursday night Camden crowd to an avant-garde dance performance. Up-

stairs in the dressing room the band was pleased as punch. "It was like an art space!" a stage-ready Beth crowed, hopping from heel to hot-pink heel.

In the cinema arts café the afternoon after the Electric Ballroom gig, the band was considerably loosened up from the first time we met, repeatedly collapsing in hoots, and listing their ultimate hard-rock hunks. (It's a toss-up between Thor Harris from Swans and Josh Homme, "the modern-day Elvis.") The hangovers may have had something to do with it. After some prodding, they admitted that their more pointed moves over our meetings for this feature—being interviewed individually, the imposing tape recorder—really just represented their lack of experience in press situations.

Still, their occasionally overprotective hold on precisely what they do is part of what makes them thrillingly different from countless young groups who tend to delight in shambolic guilelessness. Those bands can never be caught out because they don't have any beliefs to begin with. Savages may constantly contradict themselves, but they are more interesting for it. These imperious, Romantic punks want to be nothing less than a gateway drug to transformative art and ideas.

Tending hangover headaches (Milton's face was on the table more than once), Savages offered the simplest interpretation of their sound yet.

"It's music to break shit to!" laughed Thompson.

"And fuck on the floor to!" said Milton, crumpling beneath extreme-hangover hysteria.

Thompson concluded: "It's music to break shit *and* fuck on the floor to."

Savages

The Relentless Hustle of Danny Brown

BY CARRIE BATTAN

PHOTO BY EREZ AVISSAR

Danny Brown

Danny Brown is ready for his Afropunk Fest set to be over. Not because he is having a bad time. As usual, he seems thrilled. "I can't wait 'til I'm done so I can go out there with the people," he announces cheerfully, "and smoke a big-ass blunt—and I SMOOOKE!" Right on cue, "Blunt After Blunt"—from Brown's internet-fame-making 2011 mixtape *XXX*—begins to bellow through the speakers.

The rapper is on autopilot this August afternoon, cruising through a set he has tirelessly perfected over the last two years. His standard arsenal of crowd-pleasers is punctuated by his trademark tics: the devil horns thrown up high in the air, the electrocuted head-banging and hair-whipping, the lizard-like tongue spastically thrust through the toothless gap in his mouth. Unlike so many of his contemporaries, Brown appears on stage by himself, turns the vocals up high, and performs a carefully mapped sequence of full tracks. He knows exactly when to turn his microphone to the audience, and they know the right words to yell: "Ate that bitch pussy 'til she squirted like a dolphin!"

The Detroit native currently sits at the intersection of many hip-hop worlds. He is a weirdo with a traditionalist ear, a rap-nerd favorite who can make non-rap fans go crazy at festivals, a 32-year-old veteran with the kind of industry momentum typically granted to prodigies. He is someone who can work with the most brutal of Chicago street rappers [1] and then buy beats from—and befriend—a wholesome, Canadian electro-pop act like Purity Ring.

"People always looked at me, like, 'Damn, Danny crazy,' so I kinda ran with it," he tells me. "I would scare even the streetest niggas by hanging out with weird white boys and doing drugs—real killers would be like, 'What the fuck is you doing?'"

But just as listeners at large have begun to fully embrace his brand of oddballism, Danny Brown is preparing to pivot away from his madcap, lovably sex-and-drug-crazed persona with his proper debut album, *Old*, which feels practically chaste stacked up against *XXX*. The changeup could unravel some of his victories, rendering him an underdog yet again. He doesn't seem to mind.

Perched at a corner table in Williamsburg's painstakingly hip Wythe Hotel the day after playing his label Fool's Gold's Labor Day bash, Brown explains how the nonstop party of the last few years has worn down his appetite for thrills. "I've been desensitized to everything," he says. "I don't care about sex anymore. Yesterday, I told three girls: 'I'm going back to my hotel room to watch cartoons and go to bed by myself.'"

"Pre-*XXX*, I had a lot of girls, and it was fun!" he continues. "But now it's just a headache. It's hard to trust people. You talk to a girl, and then she screenshots a text message."

This spring, Brown faced a flurry of internet attention, mostly bad, after being fellated on stage by a female audience member during a performance in Minneapolis. A grainy video of the incident surfaced online, along with a spate of blog posts about rap and masculinity and faultlines. "[It] was not a thing Danny facilitated—it was an actual sexual assault," chimed in young Tumblr MC Kitty, who was opening for him on

---

[1] This refers to SD, a lesser-known member of Chief Keef's GBE cohort. Together, they made a song called "New World Order" and a video for it. Brown later told me about his experience meeting Chief Keef and GBE—even though Chief Keef is his favorite rapper, he made a point not to act like a fawning fan and instead focused his energy on SD, and expressed admiration for his music. SD was appreciative, and it led to "a collaboration." That's a perfect example of Brown's thoughtfulness and his shrewdness in navigating the industry and shaping his brand.

tour at the time. [2]

While Brown says he "loves [Kitty] like my daughter," he doesn't totally agree with her interpretation of the incident. "I look back at it and see that it takes two to tango," he admits. "As much as it was [the young woman at the concert's] fault, it was my fault, too."

Whereas *XXX* brought Brown's escapades into too-clear focus with lines like, "Stank pussy smelling like Cool Ranch Doritos," *Old* approaches sexuality and drugs from a greater distance. On an eerie, slow-burning track called "Torture", he's downcast, describing a Detroit scene from long ago: "Remember one time, dog/ This fiend owed the boss/ Put peanut butter on her pussy, let his pits lick it off." Brown, who recruited little-known London producer Paul White [3] to guide much of the album's cerebral, sample-heavy music, has also been studying up on song structure and how to fit his raps into non-traditional time signatures. [4]

On "Get Clean", a song that samples classic stoner rock, his voice is unrecognizably measured as he describes the battle against his hard-partying tendencies. "Daughter sending me messages, saying, 'Daddy, I miss you'/ But in this condition I don't think she need to see me/ Ain't slept in four days and I'm smelling like seaweed," he raps. Brown's high-school sweetheart had a child with another man 12 years ago; when she and Brown reunited afterward, he took her in as his own

child. Now that she's in sixth grade, and he's able to provide for her financially—he gives her wads of cash on occasion without telling her mother—he laments not being able to spend time with her.

"I listened to *Old* every day and thought, 'I need to make this more entertaining,'" he says of the album's meditative undertones, particularly on its front half. "But in my heart it felt right."

It's also strategic. "I don't want to be predictable," he stresses. At one point, his friend Schoolboy Q jokingly warned him that he'd risk winding up a novelty act or a punchline like Plies, a rapper known exclusively for his sexual explicitness. Brown internalized the comment, like he seems to do with so much of the information he absorbs on a daily basis. "I see everything," he says. "I'm an internet guy." Name a video, he's watched it. Mention an interview, he's read it. He is constantly taking in what goes on around him, processing it, and spinning the insight into his work and behavior.

So while the first half of *Old* marks a risky pushback against a persona that could have become a caricature, there is a calculated insurance plan built in, too. Brown closes the record out with a string of high-adrenaline electronic songs designed for maximum impact live, like a smaller-scale version of the thumping back half of Nicki Minaj's polarized *Pink Friday: Roman Reloaded*. [5] "A majority of my income comes from festivals, so I have to look at that as a business," says Brown. "Those songs are disposable in some sense, but they still have quirk. I'm not going to make a radio song, but I'll make a song that'll go off at a festival." Still, there is a plaintive current that runs through even these more hyped tracks.

ILLUSTRATION BY MICHAEL DEFORGE

---

[2] Danny retweeted this post a couple of times, which some people took as an implicit endorsement of the argument being made. I wish I had asked Danny about his Twitter habits—for someone who thinks very hard about his career, he pretty much retweets everything about himself, good or bad. He takes an anything-goes approach to his image, both in terms of promoting himself online, and granting access to media outlets. It seems like getting his name out there is more important than dictating *how* he gets his name out there, which I respect.

[3] Danny Brown discovered Paul White between *XXX* and *Old* one day when he was cleaning out his Gmail account. He thought he had pretty much given up on random beats, but decided on a whim, or some bit of cosmic serendipity, to check out what White had sent him. It worked out for both of them.

[4] You might notice how excellent the recording quality of *Old* is compared to *XXX* and *The Hybrid*. That was A-Trak's doing. "He just wanted to beef it up. He's a DJ and he understands that," Danny says. "That was his problem with *XXX*—is that it was so lo-fi and you couldn't play a French Montana or a Kanye song and then a Danny Brown song in a DJ set."

[5] Brown told me that when he was making music years and years ago—before the advent of high-quality home-recording technology— he'd save up money and take a bus to a studio in New York. It was the same studio Nicki Minaj used in her early days; they'd both sleep on the couches there.

Danny Brown

Carrie Battan *has been writing for* Pitchfork *since 2011. Her work has also appeared in* The Boston Globe, New York Magazine *online,* Slate, *and elsewhere. Born and raised in the Philadelphia area, she now lives in New York.*

"People think 'Kush Coma' is a turn-up song," Brown says, "but it's about being depressed."

Lumbering his slender 6'3" frame around a generic Irish bar in a black hoodie and oversized Adidas track pants the day before his Afropunk set [6] [7], Brown could pass for a teenage boy who recently experienced a growth spurt. He gets fired up with the gleeful excitement of a teenager, too, particularly when the topic of rap and competition within the industry is on the table. At one point, he boasts that he can rap circles around French Montana, or that he doesn't "see eye-to-eye" with Wiz Khalifa. "There are very, very few rappers I look at, like, 'Oh, shit.' It's Chief Keef and Kendrick Lamar. Earl Sweatshirt can fit somewhere in there," he says. "And I'm Kendrick Lamar's favorite rapper."

He giddily recalls his talks with Lamar in the days after that rapper's name-calling guest verse on Big Sean's "Control". The pair's conversations sound like locker-room shit talk at its finest. "We're villains! We're villlaaaaaiiiins!" he snickers, his voice reaching that unmistakable Danny Brown register. He explains that, at first, nobody seemed to catch on to the brutality of one Lamar line: "I'm usually homeboys with the same niggas I'm rhymin' with"—a subtle expression of contempt for fellow Detroit native Big Sean, the kind of major-label star who, according to Brown, wants a big pat on the back for returning to his hometown on Thanksgiving. "You give out turkeys 'cause you not around," Brown says, finishing off his second Hennessy. "I'm out there buying people packs of cigarettes, doing the dumb shit."

At times, Brown seems nearly consumed by the idea that he's the underdog. "On an independent label, you gotta do a lot of things yourself, and it's hard," he says. "You see people who don't make music as good as me with more comfortable situations." But he's still a consummate radical, energized by rebelling against institutional forces and thriving as he nips at people's heels. "I don't want to be looked at as a major label artist, you know? If you look at the world of rock, you have indie rock and you have [mainstream] rock," he explains. "I want to be the Arcade Fire or the Bon Iver of rap."

"[Many major label artists] got more money, more fans," he continues, "but bar-for-bar, they can't fuck with me. I want to get hip-hop back to a place where it ain't a popularity contest."

Which isn't to say he doesn't toy with the idea of making the leap to a bigger stage. He's now signed with the management company of Paul Rosenberg, who co-founded Shady Records alongside Eminem. In the company's offices in New York, there's a room that looks like it hasn't been updated in over a decade, its walls plastered with framed posters of 50 Cent and Em in their primes. There's a single glaring exception—a very recent, day-glo painting of a grinning Danny Brown. It hasn't been properly hung yet. Brown says Shady Records is considering him as a prospective artist for the label, and when he was introduced to Marshall Mathers himself over the summer, he told Brown he's keeping an eye out for him. "Shady Records ain't cool, though," Brown reminds himself aloud.

He is shrewd enough to know the perks and pitfalls of all sides, and for now, he's content navigating the space between them, as tricky as it can get. "I alienated myself. I can't hang around street niggas, because I'm too weird for them. And I can't hang around regular niggas, because I'm too street for them," he says, cackling. "That's my life now!"

---

[6] It wasn't just Danny Brown and I during that interview; he brought along a friend, a woman named Angelica. I didn't ask about the nature of their relationship, but I didn't get the sense that they were romantic or involved in a business sense. It was nice to have a third party who has no stakes present during an interview.

[7] At one point during the interview, Modest Mouse's "Float On" was playing at the bar. He told me that it was the inspiration for a new song he'd recorded, even though he didn't sample it directly. I told him that it's difficult for me to listen to Modest Mouse because it reminds me of particularly awkward and emotional phases during high school. "Korn is that for me," he said.

PRIMAL SCREAM

Long-running psychedelic rock 'n' roll frontman Bobby Gillespie on the music of his life: *The Jungle Book* soundtrack, Sex Pistols, the Jesus and Mary Chain, more.
By Larry Fitzmaurice

The Jungle Book OST

—

Glasgow was a big, bustling community. My dad worked in a factory and my mom worked during the day as a secretary and at a bar at night. We would walk ourselves to school, and when we came home at teatime we had to wait outside the front door for my mom to come back from work. We were poor, but when you're young, you just kind of think everyone's the same as you.

Across the street from our house, there was the Princess Cinema, so I spent a lot of Saturday mornings there. *The Guns of Navarone* turned me into a real cineaste, and I never recovered from seeing Raquel Welch in *One Million Years B.C.* I saw *The Jungle Book* too, and that soundtrack was always in my parents' house. "I Wan'na Be Like You" is a great song. I can still remember where it is in the movie.

Edison Lighthouse:
"Love Grows (Where My Rosemary Goes)"

All the families started leaving my street, and they began demolishing the houses. My whole community was destroyed; they put a highway through it. All these kids I grew up with were disappearing. Whole streets full of people suddenly became empty. My parents were holding out to get a council house in a nice area—they didn't want to go to one of the bad areas, and believe me, there are a lot of areas in Glasgow with bad shit going down.

The upside was that we had streets full of abandoned houses to play in, which was incredible. We would break into the houses, take the doors off the hinges, and build gang huts with them. Half the wallpaper would be stripped off the wall, and you'd see three different types of wallpaper underneath. It definitely had some impact on my visual sensibilities. We eventually moved to another area of Glasgow, which was traumatic. But I loved Edison Lighthouse's "Love Grows (Where My Rosemary Goes)". That song made me really happy.

5-10-15-20 *features artists talking about the music that made an impact on them throughout their lives, five years at a time. This edition features 51-year-old Primal Scream frontman Bobby Gillespie, whose latest album,* More Light, *came out in May of 2013.*

5.

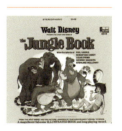

10.

15.

20.

Sex Pistols: "God Save the Queen"

—

My first interaction with punk came around this time, when I excused myself from a classroom. I said to the teacher, "I need to go to the toilet," just because I was bored. As I was walking down the stairs, there was a flier on the wall for the debate society with a picture of Johnny Rotten on it. He was on his knees, hanging onto the microphone, and his hair was all red and shredded and cut-up—he looked demonic. I just stood and looked at it. It said, "Punk rock: What does it mean?" Before I had ever heard the Sex Pistols, I saw this photograph, and I was transfixed.

In 1977, we had the Silver Jubilee and all this crazy patriotism. People wore Union Jacks and worshipped the royal family. As a kid, I fucking hated the Royal Family—I still do—so buying "God Save the Queen" felt like a real anti-authoritarian gesture. You can laugh at that 35 years later, but at the time it felt fucking powerful. John Lydon got stabbed for that song, and Paul Cook got hit with iron bars. It was quite a volatile time.

Punk did something to my mind. It really spoke to me; it was mine. If punk hadn't happened, I probably would have just had a job in a factory—quite a sad fucking life. When I started taking an interest in punk, some of the guys I was playing football with were really threatened by it. They were into Rush.

The Jesus and Mary Chain

—

I was friends with Gerard "Caesar" McNulty, and he started a band called the Wake and travelled to Manchester to give New Order's manager, Rob Gretton, a copy of their tape. Rob called a week later and said, "Would you like to support New

Order and make a record on Factory?" Everyone was blown away.

The night before the gig opening for New Order, the band's bassist disappeared. He must have shat himself or something. Caesar asked me if I could play the bass, and I said, "Yeah." Except the old bassist took his bass and amp with him. I told Rob and he said, "You're going to have to ask [New Order bassist] Peter Hook." So I go up to Hooky, who I had never met before and who was a real idol of mine, and he looked at me and said, "Fuck off!" I felt so bad. But then he went, "Of course you can use my bass, just go up on stage." Peter's bass was a Yamaha, the same one he used in the "Love Will Tear Us Apart" music video. That was incredible.

The Wake eventually threw me out in 1983. We were doing a gig supporting New Order, and I noticed that the songs were getting longer and more boring, so I just put the bass down halfway through the gig, turned it off, and walked offstage. They were mad as hell. But I wanted to play something that had more of a rock dynamic. So they sacked me.

That was the best thing that ever happened to me, though, because I went on to form Primal Scream. At that point, I was already making experimental music with Jim Beattie, and we already had the name of the band, but we didn't have a band. Around 1983, we went to a friend's club in Glasgow and told him we were looking for other band members that were into psychedelia and punk rock, and he mentioned two guys that had given him a tape a week before. It was a band called the Daisy Chain, who would eventually become the Jesus and Mary Chain. The tape had four songs on it: "Upside Down", "Never Understand", "Inside Me", and "In a Hole". It sounded incredible, so I called the number on the tape, and [former Jesus and Mary Chain member] Douglas Hart's mother answered and said he was at college, so later that night, I called him back and we spoke for two hours. I sensed a deep connection.

They had sent a demo tape to everybody in Scotland and nobody would give them a gig, so I got a guy to give them a show at a venue called

Night Moves. There weren't many people there, but it was incredible. I don't think they were on stage longer than 10 minutes. They were so wasted and smashed on booze, just colliding into each other with complete noise, chaos, and carnage. It sounded like a junkyard having a nervous breakdown, which I think was the fucking idea. The bouncers threw them off stage, and we all got thrown out of the venue. I remember going home that night and just feeling really happy inside. I had a very warm glow. I just got to see the best fucking band in the world.

I sent their tape to Alan McGee, who at this point had started a club called The Living Room in London, and he said he would give them some gigs. The band was still so nervous that, at the soundcheck, they got wasted and had an argument before they even played a note. McGee thought they were such extreme characters, and when they did play, they blew him away. He called me up and said, "I'm going to make a record with them."

Right before their first tour, the band sacked their drummer, and Alan told them that I could play drums. They called me up, and I said, "Oh, I ain't no fucking drummer." But I did it. I had never left the country up to that point, so me and Douglas went to the passport office and he said to me, "We're going to get leather trousers

and go to Germany, just like when The Beatles went to Hamburg. And when we come back, we're going to be rock 'n' roll stars." And you know what? He was right. When we came back, I bought the *NME*, and they said, "The Jesus and Mary Chain are the new Sex Pistols." I absolutely loved Jim, William, and Douglas. They were such great guys. I just felt I belonged with them. I had just as much anger as they did. The whole thing felt like a fairy tale.

In early 1986, Jim called me up one night and said, "We want you to be the full-time Mary Chain drummer, but we want you to leave Primal Scream." It really upset me, and it was a hard decision to make, because at that point I had a better time with them than I did with the Primal Scream guys. They were a better band, but I thought I was a good songwriter, too, and there would have been no outlet as a songwriter in the Mary Chain, because Jim and William were so great. That was their band.

So I decided to stay with Primal Scream, which broke my heart. I made the right decision, but I was upset about it for a long time. I went from being on tour to being back in Glasgow, playing to a couple hundred people a night. Back then, the Mary Chain had completely realized their vision. They had the whole package. The Scream didn't.

Bobby Gillespie

25.

3⊙.

Larry Fitzmaurice *resides in Brooklyn. He joined* Pitchfork *in March of 2010, where he is now Associate Editor. He has also written for* Spin, NME, GQ, *and* Tiny Mix Tapes.

Public Enemy

—

Around this time, we liked bands like Dinosaur Jr. and Sonic Youth, but generally we were a bit dissatisfied with contemporary rock music. When we discovered acid house, it made rock gigs seem old-fashioned. Also, there weren't any sexy bands—maybe Nick Cave & the Bad Seeds, but they were the only real rock stars. There was a kind of depressed atmosphere at rock gigs around that time, a subdued violence—the 1980s were a violent time in the UK, I thought, even more than the 1970s. But acid warehouse parties were illicit, illegal, underground, non-depressed, word-of-mouth, and truly subversive. There was this brand new contemporary electronic music, this new drug ecstasy, and loads of beautiful women. I was like, "Man, this is the real happening scene."

The first time I took ecstasy was in late 1988. I went to see the Happy Mondays in Brighton with Alan McGee and my ex-girlfriend, Karen Parker, who sang on The Jesus and Mary Chain's "Just Like Honey". Alan came backstage with some pills, and we took them. We kept waiting for something to happen, but nothing did.

We met [producer] Andrew Weatherall in 1989, around the time that [*Primal Scream*] came out. Alan McGee couldn't get any press to cover the album, but then Andy listed his favorite records of the summer and included "all the ballads on the new Primal Scream record." Our press agent drew our attention to it and came up with the idea of asking Weatherall to write a live feature on Primal Scream. Andy's pen name was Audrey Witherspoon, so Audrey came to review us in Exeter. We struck up a friendship and asked him to do a remix of "I'm Losing More Than I'll Ever Have", but he said, "I love the song and I wouldn't like to ruin it." We begged him to, though, and out of that came "Loaded", which was a fucking hit record. We got in the charts. It was amazing.

Alan McGee gave us a publishing advance, so we built a studio in Hackney, very near to where the Creation Records office was. Hackney has become very trendy recently, but 20 years ago, it was fucking rough. We began writing the songs for *Screamadelica*, and we learned how to use loops from listening to Public Enemy and house records. When we released it, I honestly thought it was a really cool underground rock record, like Can's *Tago Mago*. I'm not saying we were as good as Can, but I finally felt Primal Scream had made a great record that we could hold our heads up about. I didn't think it was going to be a *big* record, though. But people just love that fucking album, man.

Primal Scream:
"Give Out But Don't Give Up"

—

I don't really remember much about winning the Mercury Prize for *Screamadelica* [in 1992]—I didn't go to the ceremony. I thought the award was a load of shit and that it was weird that a telephone company was giving rock bands awards for making music. I thought the real award for making a great record was enriching people's lives. But they gave us a check for £30,000, and we lost it that night partying. We had to get our manager to call them the next day and say, "Um, we've lost the check. Can you send another one?" Then we spent that one on partying, because why not?

Making *Give Out But Don't Give Up* was hard. *Screamadelica* was such a euphoric time that there was bound to be some fallout. By 1992, a lot of the kids in the London club scene had moved on to heroin, and the band had gotten into a lot of heroin and cocaine, which affected the creative process. We stopped experimenting and just wrote a bunch of rock songs and soul ballads. The first time we attempted to make that record was at the end of 1992, and we failed because we never had any songs and everybody was doing way too much drugs in the studio. There was just complete carnage at the sessions, so Creation closed the studio down.

Skip Spence
—

This was around the time we were making *Vanishing Point*. I was listening to a lot of dub, reggae, and Skip Spence—music for psychic shipwrecks, frontier music. I thought that Skip Spence lived in a log cabin, because his music has a very old, wooden, creaking sound to it.

John Fahey
—

I had just had my first son around that time. A few years before that, I was listening to old American folk music—Harry Smith, John Fahey, the Carter Family. My wife and I had rented a little house, and we put a lot of stuff in storage, including music, so I can't remember exactly what I was listening to. I remember watching a lot of MTV, and there were a lot of garage bands from Detroit—that one band where Jack White beat one of the guys up, the Von Bondies, were all right.

Having my first son was amazing. When you leave the hospital with your baby and it's you and your wife, that's a big moment. You get in a taxi and you're holding this tiny little thing. Throughout pregnancy, it's a very abstract concept. Other people have kids, but they're not your children, so you don't have any responsibility toward them. Suddenly, you walk out of the hospital with this living being that you've got to protect and take care of and keep alive. You're like, "Whoa, here we go!"

So I had to grow up a little bit. When we recorded *Evil Heat*, we did little bits of touring,

so I partied a little on tour, but when I got home I was pretty straight. I would have a drink now and again and maybe the odd night out, but I pretty much stayed at home with my family. I was trying to learn how to balance that with being in a high-energy rock 'n' roll band. It was quite tough, like when astronauts come back to earth—I know that sounds pompous and dramatic, but it always took a week to get back into the rhythm of family life again.

Around this time, Steven Van Zandt asked Primal Scream to do a tour, but our management kept it from us because of the physical state some of the band members were in—myself included. We were all holding it together at home, but when we went on tour, it was getting really messy, and our managers felt that sending us on a 20-day tour of the States might mess things up. I have never met Steven, but I would like to meet him and clear it up, because I have a lot of respect for the man. In the last five or six years, we've straightened out and we're doing very good work. He cared about us, and I'm quite touched by that. I honestly didn't know he'd offered us that tour, because we would have done it at the fucking drop of a hat.

Deerhunter: "Monomania"
—

I love the new Deerhunter album. There's a good atmosphere to what they do. *Halcyon Digest* is more dreamy, but this one is more in your face. I've only listened to it twice, but I really like it. I think Bradford Cox is a good personality. He's kind of contentious, and I like that. He's really fucking cool. He's a character at a time when there are no characters in music anymore. Everyone is really bland, safe, conservative, and interchangeable. He stands out, and not just because he's tall.

35.

40.

50.

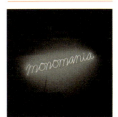

Radio-Friendly Unit Shifters

From the Cure, to Nirvana, to Limp Bizkit, to Phoenix—a look at the history of *Billboard's* Modern Rock Chart and the ever-shifting definition of "alternative."
By Chris Molanphy

ILLUSTRATION BY MICHAEL DEFORGE

In an issue dated September 10, 1988, *Billboard* quietly launched a 30-position chart toward the back of the magazine. Arriving near the end of a decade that had seen left-of-center music called everything from "post-punk" to "new wave" to "indie" to "college rock," the editors of the music-industry tip sheet went with the most neutral, business-friendly term they could think of: Modern Rock Tracks.

It was an oxymoron—a chart to track music loved by an audience that didn't want to be charted. Depending on your point of view, *Billboard* was either exceedingly late to the party or weirdly prescient. By 1988, college radio had been carving a path through youth culture for about a decade, with *CMJ* chronicling its "hits" since 1978. Punk and its immediate offshoots had come and gone. The New Romantic-driven "Second British Invasion" of the early '80s was spent as a pop force, and even second-generation punk bands Black Flag, Minor Threat, and Hüsker Dü were already broken up; so were The Smiths. Ira Robbins's *Trouser Press*, bible of left-of-the-dial music, had ceased publication four years earlier. MTV had already cycled through one late-night showcase of indie-leaning videos, *The Cutting Edge*, and was onto its second, *120 Minutes*, which launched in 1986.

On the other hand, as of September 1988, R.E.M. had just signed to a major label; Nirvana was still weeks away from issuing its first single; and Perry Farrell was merely the twitchy frontman of an LA band with a titillating album cover. The first Hot Topic store was a year away from launching. Three years before the first Lollapalooza, and well before anyone on Madison Avenue had latched onto the "A" word—before a single snide Gen-Xer had thought to ask, "Alternative to what?"—*Billboard*'s Modern Rock Tracks Chart announced that mass-market alternative culture was open for business.

Billboard was so synonymous with pop music, and the pop single in particular, that the very idea of a chart built just to track rock music was a relatively new concept. Obviously, guitar rock had been on its flagship Hot 100 pop chart for decades. But only in 1981 had the magazine begun to separately chart non-singles or "tracks"—the sorts of deep cuts that would get played on album-oriented rock radio on the FM band. By waiting until 1981 to launch its Top Tracks chart—later renamed Top Rock Tracks and, by the late '80s, Album Rock Tracks—*Billboard* missed the '70s heyday of AOR.

Modern Rock Tracks was only *Billboard's* second discrete rock chart of any kind and, like Album Rock Tracks, was an all-radio chart designed to track any song receiving spins, whether or not it was issued as a single. The chart covered a specific sliver of the radio dial, the roughly dozen college stations with large audiences, and another 18 "commercial alternative" stations (itself a relatively new category).

If nothing else, a chart like Modern Rock Tracks probably needed to exist to finally accord some music-biz stature to a slew of artists who were rock legends but had rarely graced a *Billboard* chart. Imagine you're Lou Reed or John Lydon—you've fronted bands that helped invent whole categories of rock, but you've got no million-selling albums to show for it (Lydon's work in the Sex Pistols took until the 1990s to crawl to platinum). Within a year of the Modern Rock chart launching, Reed had his first No. 1 song, and so did Lydon's Public Image Ltd. The phrase "No. 1 song" had never appeared in a sentence with these guys' names (except maybe a sentence about the Sex Pistols getting robbed of one in England).

Indeed, the whole chart felt like a cultural corrective. One look at that first Modern Rock chart in September 1988 will draw a wistful tear from anyone nostalgic for 1980s postmodern pop. The sheer variety was remarkable: reggae and rock-steady beats from the likes of Ziggy Marley, UB40, and Ranking Roger; comeback singles from 1970s punk veterans Patti Smith, Debbie Harry, and Graham Parker; coffeehouse folk from

Tracy Chapman, Toni Childs, and Joan Armatrading, alongside the pop-friendlier boho-folk of 10,000 Maniacs and Edie Brickell; Irish rock from Hothouse Flowers and In Tua Nua, and Aussie rock from INXS, Crowded House, Paul Kelly, and Hunters & Collectors. And, dominating the chart, so many gothy, dancey, eyeliner-bedecked UK acts: The Psychedelic Furs, The House of Love, The Primitives, The Escape Club, Icicle Works, Shriekback, Big Audio Dynamite, and—sitting on top like a goth godmother to all—Siouxsie Sioux, with the Banshees' "Peek-a-Boo", *Billboard's* first Modern Rock No. 1.

This list of acts doesn't just prompt nostalgia in Gen-Xers of a certain vintage. It marks the last throes of a vibrant post-New Wave music culture. That debut Modern Rock Chart offered not only eclectic music but also half-decent racial balance and strong gender balance, including a woman-fronted band at No. 1. In short, the Modern Rock Chart's first week was, arguably, the most interesting in its history. But it wasn't the last interesting week on the chart, and it definitely wasn't its cultural peak. That would come later, in the '90s, at the height of Alternative Nation.

The 25-year history of this *Billboard* chart—which since 2009 has gone by the name Alternative Songs—is punctuated by moments of deep relevance and long stretches of near-irrelevance. Even if you are now a hardcore indie-music fan who wouldn't listen to Jane's Addiction or Tori Amos even at gunpoint, chances are the bands on this chart were your gateway drugs into non-Top 40 music.

For our walk down Modern Rock Memory Lane, I've divided the chart's history into mini-eras, three to six years in length, each with a prevalent cultural theme along with a few Modern/Alternative chart-toppers that are representative of that theme. As a bonus, I am also including a special list that, um, honors a certain deathless California punk-funk band that has scored at least one No. 1 song in literally every era; rock radio programmers have been using them to fill airtime for decades. Many, *many* hours of airtime.

Chris Molanphy *is a pop-chart columnist, feature writer, and critic. He has analyzed the cross-section of art and commerce in music for two decades. In addition to* Pitchfork, *Chris's work has appeared on* RollingStone.com, Slate, Billboard, *and* CMJ. *He is a periodic guest on National Public Radio's* Soundcheck *and has appeared on* All Things Considered, Planet Money, *and* On the Media. *His book* Kurt Cobain: Voice of a Generation *was published in 2003.*

1988–1993: *The Sun Never Set on the British Empire*

KEY MODERN ROCK NO. 1s:

The Cure, "Fascination Street" (1989, 7 weeks)

Kate Bush, "Love and Anger" (1989, 3 weeks)

Peter Murphy, "Cuts You Up" (1990, 7 weeks)

Depeche Mode, "Enjoy the Silence" (1990, 3 weeks)

Jesus Jones, "Right Here, Right Now" (1991, 5 weeks)

R.E.M., "Losing My Religion" (1991, 8 weeks)

Robyn Hitchcock and the Egyptians, "So You Think You're in Love" (1991, 5 weeks)

Morrissey, "Tomorrow" (1992, 6 weeks)

New Order, "Regret" (1993, 6 weeks)

INEVITABLE RED HOT CHILI PEPPERS NO. 1:

"Give It Away" (1991, 2 weeks)

If you asked a hipster teen in 1989 or 1990 what their favorite music sounded like, they would probably point you toward something Brit-accented, wry, and a little bit mopey. No U.S. chart will ever be more dominated by limeys than the Modern Rock chart was in its first half-decade.

During this five-year period, of the 82 songs that topped Modern Rock, only 24—less than one-third—were by American acts. In 1990 and 1991 in particular, *Billboard* might as well have titled the chart "Hot Anglophile Favorites"; British and Irish acts controlled the chart for 35 weeks the former year, 41 weeks the latter (and in 1990, the chart was led by Australians—INXS, Midnight Oil, and the Church—for four more weeks). So great was the Brit hegemony that acts as quirky as Ian McCulloch, XTC, and World Party spent a month each on top.

That's not to say American acts were completely out of favor, particularly if your band was from Athens, Georgia: R.E.M. racked up four No. 1 hits in this period, The B-52's three. The Replacements stayed together just long enough into the Modern Rock era to score a sole No. 1 before imploding, and Suzanne Vega landed one before her career began its '90s downturn.

What about the breakthrough of grunge, you're wondering? Sure enough, in November 1991, Nirvana's "Smells Like Teen Spirit" hit No. 1. And then it was promptly evicted one week later, by U2's "Mysterious Ways". This is actually fairly representative of how slow-moving radio programmers reacted to The Year Punk Broke: unwilling, at first, to mess with The Cure/Depeche Mode/Morrissey axis that defined the format. As late as 1993, Pearl Jam's iconic grunge anthem "Black" was peaking at No. 20 the same week the chart was topped by a forgettable Jesus Jones song. By the end of that year, however, the pendulum began swinging away from the Brits.

1993–1996: *When Alt Became Pop*

I f you lived in New York City in the middle of 1994 and flipped your radio dial to Z100, one of the highest-rated Top 40 stations in the country, you might hear the usual Madonna and Bon Jovi fare...and then the Offspring, Veruca Salt, or Hole. This was what made the mid-1990s in America so surreal: It wasn't just that alternative music competed effectively with the middle of the road—it *became* the road. In 1987, it was possible to make your parents uncomfortable by owning a Butthole Surfers album; in 1996, you could hear that band in drive time.

Modern Rock Tracks was now, in essence, our bastard Top 40; appropriately enough, the chart expanded to 40 positions in 1994. And the music on it was way more home-grown. The shift toward American artists was swift: From 1994 to 1996, only seven British or Irish acts, total, topped Modern Rock, and one-third of these No. 1 songs were by Bush, the most American-sounding of UK acts. Britain's mope king, Morrissey, did manage to score his final Modern Rock No. 1 in 1994, but only by turning up the guitars. England's "Britpop" movement came and went, with only two Oasis No. 1s to show for it here, and a No. 2 for Elastica—no major Blur hits, and no Pulp at all. (Injustice!)

Kurt Cobain, of course, largely sparked this alt-revolution. But what has gone relatively unremarked in the received wisdom on '90s rock is that, on the radio, it was the mid-decade wave of pop-punk and alt-pop bands— not the other grunge bands—who benefited most from Nirvana's breakthrough. Pearl Jam scored a scant two No. 1 hits during alt-rock's peak ("Daughter" and "Who You Are", one week each), Soundgarden couldn't get past No. 2, and even Stone Temple Pilots found their singles stuck behind the likes of Toad the Wet Sprocket. Meanwhile, Green Day and the Offspring broke through with No. 1s in 1994 and spent the next decade and a half as radio staples.

It should be noted that women did quite well during this period: All three of Alanis Morissette's first U.S. singles reached No. 1, Juliana Hatfield and Tori Amos scored one apiece, and even Liz Phair managed a Top 10 hit. This is only notable because women artists were about to experience an appalling drought on alternative radio. After Tracy Bonham's "Mother Mother" departed the penthouse in June 1996, no solo woman would top this chart for more than 17 years; during that period, only three songs by bands with so much as a female singer (Garbage, Hole, and Evanescence) would make it to the No. 1. These stats belie the much-bandied "Lilith Era" timeline—Sarah McLachlan's all-female tour wouldn't kick off until 1997, but by that point the bro-ification of alternative radio was well underway.

KEY MODERN ROCK NO. 1s:

Nirvana, "Heart-Shaped Box" (1993, 3 weeks)

The Lemonheads, "Into Your Arms" (1993, 9 weeks)

Beck, "Loser" (1994, 5 weeks)

Green Day, "Basket Case" and "When I Come Around" (1994–95, 5 and 7 weeks, respectively)

The Cranberries, "Zombie" (1994, 6 weeks)

Live, "Lightning Crashes" (1995, 9 weeks)

Alanis Morrisette, "You Oughta Know" (1995, 5 weeks)

Bush, "Glycerine" (1995, 2 weeks)

Oasis, "Wonderwall" (1995–96, 10 weeks)

Butthole Surfers, "Pepper" (1996, 3 weeks)

Primitive Radio Gods, "Standing Outside a Broken Phone Booth With Money in My Hand" (1996, 6 weeks)

INEVITABLE RED HOT CHILI PEPPERS NO. 1s:

"Soul to Squeeze" (1993, 5 weeks)

"My Friends" (1995, 4 weeks)

1997-1999: *Faux-ternative*

What had made the mid-'90s remarkable was how alt-rock redefined what pop music could sound like. By the late 1990s, pop struck back—not just on Top 40 radio, which went scurrying away from alternative toward the loving embrace of teen-pop, but even on rock radio, where so-called alt-rock bands were essentially pop acts in tattooed-and-gelled drag. It was the last time bands like Matchbox Twenty, Third Eye Blind, and Sugar Ray could call themselves "alternative" with a straight face.

This Faux-ternative period wasn't without its pleasures; if you can resist the charms of White Town or Semisonic, you are a stronger person than I. But with the grunge explosion now more than five years in the rearview, the late '90s marked a long hangover for Modern Rock, a parade of pan-flash bands that could ride one massive radio hit to a platinum album before facing oblivion. In 1998, Marcy Playground set a then-record for longevity on the Modern Rock list with the 15-week topper "Sex and Candy"; they enjoyed one short-lived Top 10 follow up, and then were kissed off by radio programmers just one album later. The Verve Pipe, Harvey Danger, Eve 6—all gold or platinum-sellers, and all clogging up used CD bins since 1999.

(The absurdities of this period, when alt culture voraciously chewed up and spat out bands, were captured by a pair of delightful chronicles that, coincidentally, both came out in 2004 and are well worth your time: Semisonic drummer Jacob Slichter's memoir *So You Wanna Be a Rock & Roll Star*, and the documentary *DIG!* about never-was bands The Dandy Warhols and Brian Jonestown Massacre.)

However fleeting the success of these bands, at root you could still draw tenuous connections between most of their radio hits and the post-New Wave culture the Smiths and the Pixies codified. But that wouldn't last. For hints of where alternative was headed, look to a pair of Modern Rock No. 1s that bookended the late '90s—hits that now, with hindsight, seem ominous: Sublime's sun-kissed "What I Got" (late 1996, 3 weeks) and Creed's messianic "Higher" (1999, 3 weeks). Each of these relatively mellow samples of backward-ballcap rock was a Trojan Horse for the next wave to come.

1999-2002: *The Mook Shall Inherit the Earth*

Possibly the most loathed period for music of the last half-century, the rap-rock years—when looked at through the prism of the Modern Rock chart's evolution—are a logical endpoint to a decade when alt-culture steadily de-wussified itself. Fans of Kurt Cobain have long asserted that he doesn't deserve blame for the bands that kept his aggression while discarding his sensitivity, but the fact is, just as grunge gave rock radio a handy way to reassert its rebel cred in 1991, so too did Angry White Boy rock give its fans license to break with the past. Or maybe just break stuff.

This mini-era will forever be synonymous with the dreaded Limp Bizkit, but that's not entirely fair. (Just mostly fair, because after Woodstock '99, who doesn't want to blame Fred Durst for things?) The Limpsters scored one lone Modern Rock chart-topper, December 1999's "Re-Arranged", which was actually one of the less belligerent rock hits of the period. Their peers in aggro bro-itude, Korn, had an even more modest chart presence—a handful of Top 10 hits, none peaking higher than 1999's "Freak on a Leash" (No. 6) or 2002's "Here to Stay" (No. 4).

So if Korn and Limp weren't actually omnipresent on the radio at the turn of the century, why did it seem like they were? Because every other band on alt-rock radio was copping bits of their style: Papa Roach and Staind, the self-righteous self-pity; Fuel and Puddle of Mudd, the amelodic grunting; Crazy Town, the paper-thin hip-hop signifiers. (Durst himself actually mentored both Staind and PoM.) Of the lot, LA's Linkin Park distinguished itself by fusing some modest techno flourishes with the self-flagellating lyrics and crunch of rap-rock to emerge with an actual career once the fad passed.

If we can be grateful to rap-rock for anything, it's that it led to its own corrective, in the form of the garage-rock revival of the early 2000s. Unfortunately, as the nascent blog era's first major hype, nu-garage proved to be more chatter-generator than radio presence, although the "The" bands did make dents on the Modern Rock Chart. The Strokes' "Last Nite" reached No. 5; The Hives' "Hate to Say I Told You So" made No. 6; The Vines' "Get Free" hit No. 7; and The White Stripes, the fad's most enduring band, only reached No. 12 with "Fell in Love with a Girl". Jack and Meg would do better (and become more interesting) in the mid-aughts.

KEY MODERN ROCK NO. 1s:

3 Doors Down, "Kryptonite" (2000, 11 weeks)

Papa Roach, "Last Resort" (2000, 7 weeks)

Fuel, "Hemorrhage (In My Hands)" (2000–01, 12 weeks)

Crazy Town, "Butterfly" (2001, 2 weeks)

Staind, "It's Been Awhile" (2001, 16 weeks)

Nickelback, "How You Remind Me" (2001, 13 weeks)

Linkin Park, "In the End" (2001, 5 weeks)

Puddle of Mudd, "Blurry" (2002, 9 weeks)

INEVITABLE RED HOT CHILI PEPPERS NO. 1s:

"Otherside" (2000, 13 weeks); "Californication" (2000, 1 week)

"By the Way" (2002, 14 weeks)

2003-2008: *The Oligopoly*

KEY MODERN ROCK NO. 1s:

Foo Fighters, "All My Life" (2002–03, 10 weeks)

Linkin Park, "Numb" (2003–04, 12 weeks)

Incubus, "Megalomaniac" (2004, 6 weeks)

Green Day, "American Idiot" (2004, 6 weeks)

Foo Fighters, "Best of You" (2005, 7 weeks)

Incubus, "Anna Molly" (2006–07, 5 weeks)

Linkin Park, "What I've Done" (2007, 16 weeks)

Foo Fighters, "The Pretender" (2007, 18 weeks)

Incubus, "Love Hurts" (2008–09, 3 weeks)

INEVITABLE RED HOT CHILI PEPPERS NO. 1S:

"Can't Stop" (2003, 3 weeks)

"Dani California" (2006, 14 weeks)

"Tell Me Baby" (2006, 4 weeks)

"Snow (Hey Oh)" (2007, 5 weeks)

If I had to pick an absolute nadir for alternative rock as a format, it wouldn't be the maligned rap-rock years, which for all their obnoxiousness at least offered a goofy sense of misplaced conviction. No, it would be the mid-aughts—alt-rock's very own Corporate Rock era. Actually, that analogy is an insult to late-1970s rock, because even the age of Styx, Boston, and Journey offered more sonic variety. Dave Grohl is a nice guy, but I'm not sure he's written anything as enduring as "More Than a Feeling" yet.

Blame the explosion of the iPod and iTunes, which hollowed-out listenership among young men, the very consumers who fled record stores first. Rock radio programmers scrambled to retain the dudes who weren't permanently attached to white earbuds and could still be counted on to tune in. The result: a Modern Rock penthouse with a lock that, seemingly, only five American bands had the keys for: Foo Fighters, Green Day, Linkin Park, Incubus, and, yes, The Chili Peppers. During the six-year period from 2003 to 2008, this five-band oligopoly controlled the No. 1 spot 152 out of 313 weeks—a preposterous 49 percent of the time.

It was the era of the known quantity: *Any* act providing the right mix of familiarity and "edge" would be rewarded with permanent residence, and dominant songs would lodge at No. 1, or in the Top 10, for months on end. Nine Inch Nails and Weezer, two bands with respected 1990s legacies, actually had their biggest Modern Rock successes in this period, with some of their least challenging music—three No. 1s for Weezer from 2005 to 2008 (including such fan-dividers as "Beverly Hills" and "Pork and Beans"), and four straight for NIN from 2005 to 2007 (including "Every Day Is Exactly the Same"—you can say that again, Trent).

Relief came only occasionally, from rock's most palatable, blog-friendly fringes. Jimmy Eat World's two No. 1s, "The Middle" (2002, 4 weeks) and "Pain" (2004, 1 week), planted a flag for emo before Fall Out Boy and Panic! at the Disco took the movement deeper into pop. Jack White survived the garage fad to become an actual rock star, scoring No. 1s with both The White Stripes (2003's "Seven Nation Army" and 2007's "Icky Thump", three weeks each) and The Raconteurs (2006's "Steady As She Goes", 1 week). Modest Mouse's post-indie chart-topper "Float On" (2004, 1 week) still looks like a fluke a decade later, albeit a happy one. And My Chemical Romance's "Welcome to the Black Parade" (2006, 7 weeks) offered a welcome infusion of pomp and style the chart sorely needed.

2009-2013: *The Return of the New Wave*

When the history of alt-rock is written, maybe Phoenix's "1901" should be accorded as much respect as "Smells Like Teen Spirit". Though it's not as great of a song, in terms of culture shifts, all Nirvana did at the turn of the 1990s was move alternative radio away from some pretty cool British bands toward a bunch of American ones. Phoenix, at the turn of the 2010s, arguably helped save alt-rock radio from itself.

Phoenix's slow-breaking hit—it was released in February 2009 but reached No. 1 a full year later—had the hallmarks of a driving guitar jam. But it was also the New-Waviest and, bluntly, girliest song to top the chart *Billboard* now called Alternative Songs in quite some time. True, Coldplay had already cracked alt-rock's façade with their florid, poppy "Viva la Vida", which reached No. 1 two summers earlier (2008, 2 weeks). But Coldplay were by then radio superstars being grandfathered in, and they didn't do much to shift the chart's direction. Phoenix were new, an acclaimed indie band (on mega-independent Glassnote Records), and they were French, for crying out loud.

Alternative Songs didn't change overnight after Phoenix went to No. 1—plenty of turgid *rawk* continued to command the list. But the tempo and tone of the songs making the upper reaches began to evolve in an indier, even poppier direction. And some new chart-toppers, like Mumford & Sons' "Little Lion Man", were probably better suited to a hoedown than the radio.

By 2011, however, the Alternative chart began doing something it hadn't done since the '90s: break new acts at Top 40 radio. Foster the People's "Pumped Up Kicks" was the year's top Alternative hit and a Top Three hit on the Hot 100. In 2012, for the first time ever, *Billboard*'s No. 1 Hot 100 song of the year and top Alternative song of the year were the same: Gotye's airy, lovelorn ballad "Somebody That I Used to Know"—the kind of ornate, mopey record alt-rock radio would have played to death in its late-1980s, pre-Nirvana salad days. Back then, only a few Modern Rock hits were shared with Top 40 radio. Now, the Gotye song fit on both ends of the dial, along with fun.'s "Some Nights", and Alex Clare's "Too Close", and Capital Cities' "Safe and Sound".

The ultimate sign that the Alternative chart has come full circle to the early days of Modern Rock Tracks? A woman is finally No. 1. In August, Lorde's "Royals" became the first chart-topper by a solo female artist since Tracy Bonham in 1996, appropriately timed for the 25th anniversary of a chart that launched with Siouxsie Sioux's record in the top slot. But is "Royals" a great moment for women, or a great moment for an "alternative" culture that long, long ago became middle-of-the-road? Does it even guarantee we won't have to hear another phoned-in Red Hot Chili Peppers song during drive time? Nah—but if it means commercial alt-rock radio, or this chart, can resume its place as our bastard Top 40, we'll take it. ✏

KEY MODERN ROCK NO. 1s:

Kings of Leon, "Use Somebody" (2009, 3 weeks)

Muse, "Uprising" (2009–10, 17 weeks)

Phoenix, "1901" (2010, 2 weeks)

The Black Keys, "Tighten Up" (2010–11, 10 weeks)

Cage the Elephant, "Shake Me Down" (2011, 6 weeks)

Foster the People, "Pumped Up Kicks" (2011, 5 weeks)

Gotye featuring Kimbra, "Somebody That I Used to Know" (2012, 12 weeks)

fun., "We Are Young" and "Some Nights" (2012, 2 weeks and 3 weeks, respectively)

Alex Clare, "Too Close" (2012, 4 weeks)

The Neighbourhood, "Sweater Weather" (2013, 11 weeks)

Lorde, "Royals" (2013, 4 weeks to date)

INEVITABLE RED HOT CHILI PEPPERS NO. 1S:

"The Adventures of Rain Dance Maggie" (2011, 4 weeks)

OUR OWN SENSE OF TIME

How Vampire Weekend's new album rescues the term "millennial" from overzealous cultural pundits as it evades nostalgia in favor of a faithful present. **By Lindsay Zoladz**

A couple of years ago, when I had one of those desk jobs where you have time to sit around and read the internet all day, I had two favorite pastimes: reading articles about "millennials," and cringing at them. Like a lot of my peers, I've always had an uncomfortable relationship with the M-word, and even now my fingers cramp up when I try to type it without using a protective force field of scare quotes. I don't think I have ever met anyone who self-identifies as a "millennial," and when people my age (26) hear the word, it generally strikes us as a story being written without our consent—like a cheesy made-for-TV movie about our lives. But, with or without our approval, it seems like a new one of these articles crops up every other day, an endless series of jabs at the pause button, each one trying to capture a more perfectly composed freeze-frame of *right now*. They are usually written by people from previous generations and published in places like *The New York Times* and *The Los Angeles Times* and *Time*. I even have a recollection of one in Amtrak's seatback magazine, illustrated by a dynamic photo of a Cool Millennial Dude in sneakers and a business suit, breakdancing on a conference table.

I remember this last one vividly because I read it on a momentous occasion: the first business trip of my "adult" life. In this case, the scare quotes are there to indicate that I had to sheepishly phone home and borrow money from my parents to front the cost of the train ticket until my office reimbursed me. And yet, even as I sat there acting out a real-life Lena Dunham punchline, I still remember coming to the end of this Amtrak article about "millennials in the workplace" and thinking: "This isn't me, exactly."

This was 2010, the year I first felt my sense of time breaking down completely. It was, not coincidentally, the first year I had a desk job and thus the first year I spent eight-plus hours a day in front of a screen. The days lapsed in disorienting flickers in the bottom right hand of my screen: 9:51 am turning to 12:33 pm and somehow to 5:36 pm in what seemed like a couple of blinks. But even when I looked up from my monitor, a shift seemed to be occurring on a larger scale, too.

For one thing, the nostalgia cycle was all out of whack. The 1990s were back, but simultaneously so were the 1980s, and the 1970s, and the 1960s—and the 1890s. Mythic records and out-of-print cult movies I had spent half my life searching for were now available in a single, anticlimactic click, and the Willy Wonka-brite buffet of the internet meant everybody was gorging on the recent past, but perhaps at the expense of the present. The wheels of time started to resemble a jammed cassette: The past was coiling over on itself in such a tangle that it didn't feel like there was much room for the present. And maybe that was part of the reason why I found the vague idea of "millennials" so difficult to identify with, to claim as my own.

Accordingly, as a music fan, 2010 was the year I really started to worry about losing the thread. It was easy to describe what 1991 or 1994 or even 1999 "sounded like," but what did 2010 sound like? Even in retrospect, would it have any solid identity? Did it need to? In time, would the expectation of "progress" become an outdated relic? Music critic Simon Reynolds's 2011 book *Retromania* thoughtfully addressed these and plenty of related questions, and though his tone was encouragingly hopeful (spoiler: the last line of the book is, "I still believe the future is out there"), I just as often found myself mulling over a quote he included from the computer scientist Jaron Lanier's polemic *You Are Not a Gadget*: "Play me some music that is characteristic of the late 2000s as opposed to the late 1990s." I constantly updated a mental list of things I would play Lanier to prove him wrong—Nicki Minaj! Flying Lotus! The Weeknd! Rustie! Frank Ocean! Grimes!—but the truth is that deep down, exhausted by unimaginative revivalists and photocopied nostalgia, a skeptical voice nagged in my head almost constantly: *Maybe it is true. Maybe there is nothing new under the sun anymore.* Until 2013, which is when, rather abruptly, I once again started believing in right now.

"I'm a senior at Yale, graduating in May, and I'm terrified," wrote a student named Bijan Stephen in an op-ed published on *Quartz* this past spring. It was a sentiment shared by countless,

Ordinary Machines *is a column by Lindsay Zoladz about the ways music, technology, and identity intersect in the 21st century.*

decidedly less publicized Tumblr rants. The article's title was a play on a song he proposed as a kind of generational anthem, a track off Vampire Weekend's 2008 debut album, "The Kids Don't Stand a Chance".

When Vampire Weekend put out that first record, the term "millennial" was already in use (it goes all the way back to 2000, when Neil Howe and William Strauss published the book *Millennials Rising*), but it wasn't nearly as ubiquitous or exhaustively debated as it is right now. In this moment of SEO-crazed "content creation" and click-bait contrarianism, millennials have become the new milk: one minute their iconoclasm and disillusionment and dogged self-aggrandizement is good for society, the next they are said to be corroding its very skeleton with their selfies and parents' basement apartments and inextinguishable sense of entitlement. (Somehow the exclamatory title of this recent *Salon* op-ed speaks volumes about think-piece fatigue: "I Don't Hate Millennials Anymore!") So earlier this year when Vampire Weekend put out their third album *Modern Vampires of the City*—a record that dares not only to take the Lord's name in vain but to pitch-shift it, and to deliver such shruggingly anthemic lines as "I'm not excited, but should I be?/ Is this the fate that half of the world has planned for me?"—it was inevitable that fans and critics alike would try to make the M-word stick to it.

I'm not sure which surprises me more: the fact that the band hasn't really tried to shake the word off (when faced with the term "millennial unease" in a recent Pitchfork interview, frontman Ezra Koenig replied with a laugh: "I like that phrase. It's a concise way to describe a lot of the feelings on the album."), or the fact that talking about this record has marked one of the first times in my life that I don't feel entirely icky using it. Maybe that's because—although it is obviously meticulously crafted—*Modern Vampires'* aphorisms feel so nonchalant that their resonance comes off like a happy accident. It is not a political record, but it specifically captures something elusive about what it feels like to come of age in an era that is si-

multaneously hopeful and post-HOPE, and when the limitlessness of the internet has become so thoroughly internalized that any direct talk about it runs the risk of being unforgivably cheesy.

So the slyest—and maybe smartest—thing about the omnivorously referential *Modern Vampires* is that it manages to be earnest but never *too* on the nose. Chief arranger Rostam Batmanglij envelops the music in a dense-yet-airy fog, which provides the perfect foundation for Koenig's lyrics, which are at once hyper-articulate and playfully evasive. "The perfect tone is halfway between deeply serious and totally fucking around," Koenig said, pointing specifically to the single "Diane Young". The band thought about calling the song "Dying Young", but quickly decided to go with a cheeky homophone instead; "Dying Young" sounded "so heavy and self-serious." And maybe that seemingly tiny pivot is the most profoundly millennial thing about it. How do you make a record about post-ironic characters who cringe at the phrase "post-irony," a record that sneakily defines a generation that is always going to approach something generation-defining with an air of "this isn't me, exactly?" The answer may exist somewhere in the space between dying young and "Diane Young".

Both sonically and lyrically, the album is richly panoramic, but one particular thing that strikes me every time I listen is how often it references time. From the persistent second hand tick in "Don't Lie" to the way the refrain "there's a lifetime right in front of you" becomes, in a flicker as unceremoniously devastating as a lost afternoon lapsed on a digital clock, "there's a headstone right in front of you." There's something strange, illogical, and uneasy about the way time passes on this record; you could definitely say it's on some Benjamin Button shit. Koenig's characters age erratically ("young hips shouldn't break on the ice") or live, stubbornly, forever ("hold me in your everlasting arms"), but it is a testament to Batmanglij's vision that you feel this tug-of-war between past and future on a wordless, gut level too. We are living, as the writer Michelle Orange observes in her very good new

PHOTO BY KYLE DEAN REINFORD

essay collection, *This Is Running for Your Life*, "in a time that is no time and only time and all times, all the time." *Modern Vampires* renders exactly what that sounds like and acknowledges it as a perfectly good reason for an identity crisis. Somewhere between the lines, though, it also reassures—"oh, sweet thing"—that this is not the end of the world: to some extent, things have always been this way. Time marches on.

The album's centerpiece (and my favorite song of the year so far), "Hannah Hunt", feels simultaneously hyper-modern and timeless. It's about the allure of going off the clock and off the grid, which might seem like a distinctly 2013 concern to somebody who has never read *Walden* or heard "Born to Run". So maybe the only new thing about "Hannah Hunt" is its context—that it sees human connection as a potential relief from today's *no time and only time and all times, all the*

time. It's a break-up song, and a devastating one at that, but in this four-minute world, love is both a freeze frame amidst the rush and a belief in the primacy of the present: "You and me, we got our own sense of time."

Last month, two of my friends got married and, as everyone moved from an antiquarian, marble-surfaced atrium to the adjacent reception hall, one of the first songs they played was Vampire Weekend's "Step". "Wedding DJs playing Vampire Weekend!" seems like a detail someone might include, with outsized anthropological significance, in an article about millennials getting married—though, if I were to read something like it now, my response would be, "Well, yeah. And… ?" Sometimes it takes a record to clarify something very obvious, and in this case it's an idea—our present is just as good as your past. 🖋

Lindsay Zoladz *is an associate editor at* Pitchfork, *where she writes a column called Ordinary Machines about her ambivalent relationship with technology. Her writing has also appeared in* The Believer, Slate, Salon, Bitch, *and more. She lives in Brooklyn.*

Shaking Through: Music and Mania

ILLUSTRATION BY MICHAEL DEFORGE

One writer's struggle with
an idiosyncratic, anxiety-based
condition called psychomotor agitation.
By Jayson Greene

Overtones *is a column by Jayson Greene that examines how certain sounds—a snare crack, a synth blob, a ghostly string sample—linger in our minds and lives.*

f you have ever spotted me on the street and walked up to say hi, there is a good chance you stopped yourself before reaching me. My mouth is working slightly, you notice, and I am wearing earbuds. Maybe I'm singing to myself? Then you see my right hand at my side, holding my house keys and twitching spasmodically. *Hmm*, you think, *maybe now is not the best time*.

This happens constantly. Longtime friends and acquaintances are likely used to it. As I smoothly pocket my keys, as if they had stopped me in the middle of doing something normal, there is no acknowledgment between us, no "what are you doing there?" Still, in my more self-conscious moments, I picture a conversation between two coworkers, comparing notes later in the day: What the hell *is* that?

Well, there are a lot of names for "that." Twitching, spazzing: those aren't the kindest, but they are descriptive. I stumbled across a longer, more official name last year while doing some idle self-diagnosis. "Psychomotor agitation: a series of unintentional, purposeless motions that stem from mental tension and anxiety." Reading it, I felt a small "alternate history" chill run backward over my childhood. Ah. So *that*'s what that is.

I am exceedingly lucky: Other sufferers bite the flesh off their fingertips, bang their heads into walls, knock things over. My "purposeless motion" has always been benign. In a word, I shake. I have been shaking things my entire life. When I was old enough to close my baby fist around something, I selected a piece of rubber tubing, broken off a larger toy, and whipped it around. Eventually, I settled on socks—pliable, soft, one for each hand, always readily available. I balled one up in each of my little hands, and shook them, furiously. For hours. I paced, I muttered; my socks whirled, mostly noiselessly, around me. When I was seven, my father filmed me doing it. [1]

So that's what I'm doing. But what the hell am I *doing*? On the rare occasions when I have mustered the courage to talk about it, or gotten drunk enough, my story tends to leave my listeners looking at me blankly. "Shaking my socks" confounds people's understanding of basic sentence structure: You *what* your *what*? [2]

What I know for certain is that this bizarre behavior is inextricably linked to my relationship to music. My mind is a paint can; music is an automatic mixer. Music that worries away at, or endlessly embroiders, a single nagging thought, like Steve Reich, feels oddly familiar and comfortable to me: There is something pre-cognitive in it, a shape as old and recognizable as my mother's breath rising in her chest. [3]

The high-speed velocity of thrash metal or hardcore punk was the same. Bad Brains' self-titled album caromed off its own edges, charging forward through the universe with a liberating

---

[1] Looking back, I am struck with admiration for my parents' very "I'm OK; You're OK" approach to a tic that might have alarmed many. The only perhaps-unfortunate side effect of this treatment, however, was that it allowed the behavior to take root and linger: The sight of a seven-year-old pacing around telling himself stories with his socks in his hand. Cute? Imagine a teenager doing the same thing, late at night, withdrawing socks from under couch cushions after the family was asleep. *Less* cute.

[2] When this piece was published, I wondered, idly, if other sock-shakers would step forward, their eyes shining, their voices husky expounding: "I thought I was the only one." Not so. Google "shake my socks" and marvel at the gap in the known behavioral universe.

[3] Part of preparing this piece involved mental-disorder research—a slightly morbid exercise that nonetheless propelled me down some interesting side paths. One detail I left out of the original piece because it seemed too knotty to address properly in the space of the column: "psychomotor agitation" isn't considered a disorder—it's more a smattering of *symptoms*. More telling: it's a symptom classified under the mental illness "bipolar 2."

Now, I don't suffer from bipolar disorder: Reading about the sufferings of people diagnosed with true bipolar disorder gave me a private sense of relief, that sort of shameful "things could always be worse" feeling that people don't talk about because it feels small. But I did find myself reading an awful lot about the relationship between hypomanic episodes and earworms. As a music critic, I have a congenial relationship with my earworms; I imagine that life without them would be as unbalanced and miserable as life without my gut bacteria.

"I was much more easily overwhelmed when I was a child. Back then, anything—a new tape, a new comic book, a cartoon—would send me into hours of paroxysms."

urgency I immediately identified with. I had no aggression, no politics. I didn't hate the cops or Ronald Reagan or want a safe place to skate. I loved this music because it felt like shaking, bottled. When I heard that sound, my world doubled in size. It certainly felt that way at the time, but looking back, I have asked myself if the music I love shaped my mind or if my mind went looking for congenial shapes, companions that told me something I already knew.

With rap, it was the pure sensory overload of all the words that first enticed me. Here was all this *information*, spilling out in a hopeless tumble, all of it urgent and streaming forth faster than anyone could hope to catch it. I have always had a special place in my heart for verbose, excitable rappers—E-40, or Big Boi. Their words emerged spring-loaded, compressed, thoughts stacking relentlessly on top of each other. (When my parents took me to a counselor, in my teens, it was because they had noticed I was exhibiting "pressured speech," or "a tendency to speak rapidly and frenziedly, as if motivated by an urgency not apparent to the listener." When I was in fifth grade, I spent a few months with a speech therapist, correcting a stutter that I explained to the woman felt like "all the words in my sentence trying to get out the door at the same time.")

In short, I appreciate urgency. There has always been too much to do, too much to take in, at any given moment, from any fixed place in the world. I was much more easily overwhelmed when I was a child. Back then, anything—a new tape, a new comic book, a cartoon—would send me into hours of paroxysms. How was I expected to sit still when there was this much energy coursing through the air? The shaking gathered in me like a lightning storm, a neural sneeze. It was impossible to deny.

I am still powerless over this impulse when a piece of music taps into that place in me. If I leave work with a new rap song ringing in my ears, the chain reaction starts. Instantly, I am envisioning the arc of a rapper's career: Their earliest mixtape-and-flyer days, their diligently cultivated local fan base, their eventual big break. I thumbnail-sketch their moment in the pop-cultural sun, their one or two major label-financed records with their one or two respectably performing pop singles. There are cameo parts for the pop culture wonks cracking jokes about their catchphrases, the clubs that would play them 10 years later to the cheers of nostalgic college kids. I even imagine their entrepreneurial side businesses—a food franchise, maybe, with seven locations. By this time, I have made the seven minute walk from my office to the subway. I look down. My keys are gripped tightly in my hand. I might as well have been deposited on another planet, so far away am I from my starting point.

I keep my keys off a keychain most of the time now. It doesn't matter if I keep them zipped in the bottom of my bag like the dry-drunk alcoholic who eventually goes for the mouthwash, I know I will inevitably go scrabbling for these small pieces of metal. It is a humbling, and mortifyingly silly, addiction. Once, reaching for my keys while standing at a subway platform, I accidentally grabbed and flung them onto the train tracks, all in one frantic motion. I locked eyes with an alarmed and uncomprehending fellow commuter as the train passed over them, but could offer no explanation. As usual, I was wearing earbuds. In a perfect world, I would have gestured to them and he would have understood. It's not my fault, I would say. Have you *heard* this stuff? ✐

Jayson Greene *is Managing Editor at* eMusic *and a contributing editor and columnist at* Pitchfork. *His writing has appeared in the* Village Voice, BuzzFeed, GQ.com, XXL, Myspace, *and* NewMusicBox. *He lives in Brooklyn.*

ASTRAL YEARS

One writer's love-hate relationship
with Van Morrison's *Astral Weeks.*
By Mike Powell

ILLUSTRATION BY MICHAEL DEFORGE

I am 15 years old and Van Morrison's *Astral Weeks* is the worst music I have ever heard in my life. Worse than Jewel, worse than the soundtrack to *Cats*, even worse than "Brown-Eyed Girl", a song our local oldies station plays whenever I get into my mom's car, where I sink into the passenger seat with shame as she sings along: "Makin' love in the green, green grass/ Behind the stadium with you."[1] I only bother listening to *Astral Weeks* at all because my best friend loves it, and my instinct is to try and feel as much of what he feels as possible. At 15, this is one of the ways we create safety: the more we have in common, the less alone we are.

So he plays *Astral Weeks* in his busted silver Nissan and the carpeted bedroom on the second floor of his dad's house, and he gives me that expectant look people give you when they are trying to use music to communicate something they can't in their own words, using it to try to build a bridge between you and them. I sit cross-legged on the carpet and listen, waiting for all these terrible lines about ballerinas to resonate in the pit of my horny and frustrated soul—waiting, in short, to understand. It takes another 15 years.

To a white suburban punk with an almost-puritanical allergy to anything you could call "expressive," Morrison's music is a true enemy: earnest, mysterious, and committed to revelation. It's like The Doors, but harder to make fun of.[2] Every time he wails, I have bad flashbacks to the cantors at my synagogue, with their stale-smelling beards and messages of love, welcoming me into their understanding arms.

It is possible I am afraid of music as warm as Morrison's for the same reason I am afraid to tell the psychologist my school has forced me to see how I "really feel." But at 15, I think of myself as being acutely able to separate truth from bullshit,

which seems to be *everywhere*.

Morrison recorded *Astral Weeks* in 1968. He was 23. He was also broke, dejected, just married, and a new resident of Cambridge, Massachusetts, where he lived in a street level apartment with no phone and a mattress on the floor. A few months earlier, he had fulfilled a bad contract for a label called Bang Records by improvising 31 songs in a little over a half hour. One of them is about ringworm; another is about danishes.[3] It insulted everybody involved, especially Van Morrison. At one point, he was legally forbidden from playing or recording in New York; at another, the label owner's wife tried to have him deported.

Nobody who played on the sessions for *Astral Weeks* has anything nice to say about the experience. Morrison reportedly recorded all his parts in one booth—while the rest of the musicians recorded in another. Drummer Connie Kay, a longtime member of the Modern Jazz Quartet, said Morrison told him to play whatever he wanted; Richard Davis, a jazz bassist credited as the de facto bandleader, said Morrison never even introduced himself.

Part of what is remarkable about *Astral Weeks* is that you don't hear any of this in the music. You don't hear the frustration, the bitterness, or the cynicism that can so easily ferment in people when things don't go their way. You don't hear the physical alienation of the players, who seem to circle Van Morrison like a wreath of roses.

Received wisdom about the album is that it dissolved boundaries between soul, R&B, folk, and jazz. Its eight songs—four of which are over seven minutes long—don't obey rules in the way other songs do. They don't evolve so much as double back on themselves, retracing lines and melodies for minutes at a time. Listening to them is like watching a black-and-white image become

Secondhands *is a column that examines music of the past through a modern lens.*

---

[1] I am Jewish; everything my mother does embarrasses me; everything I do inspires either oppressive pride or oppressive concern. This is our way.

[2] My often-repeated but rarely accepted theory about The Doors is that they're much better if you start thinking of them as a comedy band, which by *The Soft Parade* gets almost too easy.

[3] Though obviously recorded with a minimum amount of effort for a maximum amount of insult, parts of the sessions—especially "Goodbye George"—stand as good evidence that Van Morrison probably had a harder time trying to be goofy than trying to be profound.

steadily flooded with color: The architecture of the music is there from the first second, but the songs become clearer and more vivid as they go on.

I can understand what I didn't like about the album when I was younger, but in retrospect, *Astral Weeks* has a meditative, almost autistic intensity that I have always loved in music. It is the same quality I hear in newer albums like *The Money Store* by Death Grips or *Impersonator* by Majical Cloudz, or why I prefer *Yeezus* to *My Beautiful Dark Twisted Fantasy*: They are obsessively narrow statements that fuel the myth of the artist as someone who is *not* well-rounded, who is *not* capable of seeing all points of view or transcending the confines of their own perspective—basically, the myth of the artist as someone who has yet to transform from a child into an adult. [4]

Audiences can appreciate this myth because they have probably experienced flashes of romantic single-mindedness, too. But it is also that life in its variety and responsibilities—doesn't give us much room to *be* single-minded, and so we need to step sideways into the parallel universe of art, where we are allowed to feel those narrow teenage feelings, at least for the duration of the album.

In drafting this column, I wrote paragraph after paragraph about all the albums that Morrison released after *Astral Weeks*; about the resplendent "Linden Arden Stole the Highlights" from *Veedon Fleece*; about Morrison's transition from the loose sounds of *Astral Weeks* into the tight, full-band R&B of *Moondance*; about how by the 1974 live album *It's Too Late to Stop Now*, even the digressions of "Cyprus Avenue", a pillar of *Astral Weeks*, had turned into a coordinated rave-up that Morrison used to end his concerts, a song about the freedom and confusion of adolescence performed with the control of a showman.

I wrote about the 1980s, too; about how Morrison continued to record great, despicably uncool albums like 1982's *Beautiful Vision*—albums that seem unconcerned with appealing to anyone besides Van Morrison. I wrote about how part of the fun of getting into an artist like Van Morrison or Stevie Wonder, or Prince, or anyone who seems like an open-and-shut case until you find out they had a reggae phase, or are actually still alive—isn't just listening to the masterpiece, but the 30-something albums that came after it, most of which have no reputation at all. [5]

But I kept coming back to *Astral Weeks*. To say a record came out in 1968 is a matter of historical fact, but the reality is that records come out whenever people hear them first.[6] Having been born in 1982, the year 1968 is an abstraction to me. At best, I can read a book about it, or talk about it with my parents. But in the context of my own experience, *Astral Weeks* was released around 1998, along with Aaliyah's "Are You That Somebody?", *Brighten the Corners* by Pavement, Brahms's fourth symphony, and a mixtape from my friend Meghan Kennedy, plastered in butterfly stickers and filled end-to-end with funk songs I still don't know the names of.

Because I am someone who sometimes gets paid to write about music, people like to ask me what I'm listening to now. I know they want to hear about new music, but what I really want to tell them is that it's always the music that I have been listening to for the longest time, regardless of whether I like it or not, that seems newest to me. I want to tell them that *Astral Weeks* makes a lot more sense to me in the context of an album like Animal Collective's *Sung Tongs* or the seemingly infinite loops of a Todd Terje track than anything else from 1968. I want to tell them that at 15, the album was a catalog of feelings I was

---

[4] I think you could probably argue this about most art, at least on some level; art tends to come from a part of us that isn't concerned with judgment or utility—two qualities that I associate pretty strongly with adulthood.

[5] My favorite of these is *Beautiful Vision*, whose cover depicts a rainbow beaming through some kind of crystal ball, whose first song truly earns its place on Wikipedia's "List of nontraditional bagpipe usage," whose second explores the struggle to remove psychological veils in a world of illusions through the use of lightweight disco, and whose sixth, "Cleaning Windows", is about cleaning windows. The implicit contrast in Morrison's music—between the earthly and the otherworldly—rarely got clearer.

"To say a record came out in 1968 is a matter of historical fact, but the reality is that records come out whenever people hear them first."

too afraid to have; at 30, it is a catalog of feelings I can't ever have again.

It is December 2012 and I am walking through light winter rain down 17th Street between 6th and 7th Avenues in Manhattan, listening to *Astral Weeks* on my headphones. Good-looking people shiver together on the sidewalk outside a corner restaurant. I used to live here. When I was a kid, the corner restaurant was a cheaper corner restaurant, and the brick apartment building next door was a parking lot. The day I made it to the end of the block on my bike without training wheels, the lot attendants called out my name, clapping, "Miguelito, Miguelito."

"Cyprus Avenue" comes on. In it, Van Morrison is 14 years old and in love. His girl comes down the lane on white horses with rainbow ribbons in her hair, attended by a harpsichord player who seems incapable of staying on beat. When he finally slides into step with the rest of the band, my neck hair prickles with excitement: It is the sound of someone finding their way back to where they belong.

I get a call from the friend who introduced me to *Astral Weeks* 15 years earlier. He wants to know if I want to celebrate his cousin's 24th birthday. We will go to city parties and do drugs and stay up all night. "Why not?" I tell him. We used to spend every weekend at each others' houses; now we only see each other about twice a year. Two or three hours later I am standing in the corner of a crowded loft while someone in skinny jeans and a parka screams in my face about how French Montana is the future of rap. I am sweating, I am laughing, I am thinking of a lyric from "Sweet Thing": "I will never grow so old again." ✍

Mike Powell *is a writer who lives in Tucson, Arizona.*

—

[6] If I could only be heard by the world on a single argument, this would be it. One of my greatest joys as a listener is having the experience of hearing something recorded 10 or 20 or sometimes 80 years ago and thinking *I have been looking for music like this my entire life.* Time-based narratives—the kinds that suggest that one moment begets another begets another—have never been as interesting to me as connections made between concepts and feelings, like when you realize that, say, early digital dancehall is as spare and tough as early hardcore. Suddenly sounds become metaphors and the whole listening experience opens up in new ways—and suddenly music from the past just becomes a whole new set of opportunities for connections and discovery that seem as fresh as anything that came out yesterday.

It's Just a Cassette

On the day before Cassette Store Day 2013, a meditation on the merits of the cassette tape.
By Nick Sylvester

ILLUSTRATION BY MICHAEL DEFORGE

You are not wrong to have doubts about Cassette Store Day. Though there are no proper cassette stores to speak of, there will be events in New York, Chicago, London, Fullerton, Portland, Stockholm, and other cities to celebrate the forsaken magnetic medium, 50 years after the format was invented. I run a label that sells cassettes, am co-hosting the New York event, and understand why you might think this is the biggest trolling of the music world since chillwave. But cassettes—the whole cassette thing—are not bullshit. I feel compelled to tell you why.

My reasons are entirely personal, vaguely mathematical, and probably nonsensical. The grad students among you will be disappointed to find no discussion of a "living, breathing medium that deteriorates with every play."[1] Digital has the cassette beat on portability, sharability, durability, ease of recording, etc. Vinyl—looking past the conspicuous consumption aspect, or the fact that record plant people are largely unreliable assholes[2]—whups the lowly cassette on nearly all things sonic, speaking personally. The ritual of sitting down for the sole purpose of listening to a

[1] This was perceived as a potshot. As an advanced degree holder in "The Classics"—don't drop the 'the'—I assure you I mention this conversion only with love and empathy.

[2] For small labels, I recommend the entirely decent folks at GZ Media in the Czech Republic and Gotta Groove in Cleveland.

record on vinyl, that's a special thing too.

But there is no format more human than the cassette. No format wears our stain better. I have not encountered a technology for recorded music whose physics are better suited for fostering the kind of deep and personal relationships people can have with music, and with each other through music. This sounds like nostalgia[3]—or a hipster Mitch Albom—but I don't think it is. I am talking about new music, on cassettes, in 2013. No audio format keeps me more focused on listening to the thing itself, without the distraction of having a web browser right in front of me, without the baggage of an ersatz music news cycle, the context upon context, the games of the industry. Music released on cassette does not feel desperate or needy or Possibly Important. It tends not to be concerned about The Conversation. It resists other people's meaning. That is what I like about the cassette. It whittles down our interactions with music to something bare and essential: two people, sometimes more, trying to feel slightly less alone.

Two stories. I started writing record reviews in 2002. I was in college; I loved new music. Writing about new music was a way to get records before anyone else. Easy enough. In hindsight, I underestimated how much the simple act of writing about music would rewire my brain and alter my relationship with it. I listened differently than before. The euphemism was "I was listening smartly." But all that meant was I listened for good sentences. I read music like a text, but wasn't exactly hearing it anymore. Deliberately misunderstanding something often made the writing better, and I did that a lot too. I abstracted music into ideas about music. Slowly the latter became more important to me than the music itself. I also became an incorrigible asshole, but

that's a story for a different piece. I never hated music, and I loved writing about it. But I came to resent *how* I was listening.

Second story. At the tail end of all that, I started making music again. There was something liberating about how immediate and elemental the whole thing was. No context. Pure id. A rock band when nobody cared about rock bands. We played shows in costumes. Our friends were exceedingly kind. Then people started caring about rock bands. A slew of totally well-meaning people wanted to take us to "the next level" and "build a team" and so on. It was exciting, because for a moment it seemed like this might be a Real Thing. We went on tours with great bands, made our records, played amazing shows. From all angles, things were going super well. But I also felt anxious pretty much all the time. Everything seemed to matter, down to the shoes we wore on stage.

I became intimately aware, too, of all the ugly industry machination—I'd rather not shit where I eat. If music had once been a writing exercise, now it was a hunger game, with strategies that changed by the hour and a never-ending supply of supposedly make-or-break moments that might—*might*—one day land us a mid-afternoon slot at some music festival. The entire setup of the music industry—from the gross amount of power wielded by publicists, to the convenient myth that musicians need to tour tour tour, next level next level next level—seemed to benefit everyone except the people making the music. I only saw the wires now. I felt myself becoming cynical.

Cassettes are my detox. A way for me to sidestep everything about music that isn't music.[4] To get back to the very basic propositions of why I make and listen to music in the first place.

---

[3] The Nostalgia Angle, related to the physical angle, starts from a mighty sour premise that people only truly love "the" music they heard as teenagers. It extends, most tenuously, to the idea that people most appreciate the formats they grew up with too. For my part, I listened to a shitload of Mephiskapheles and can assure you ska is not my one true love. I was also born in 1982, which means I have no nostalgia for the cassette. I always bought CDs and would sooner save up than settle. Cassettes are not nostalgic for me. Nostalgia is buying Limp Bizkit's *Three Dollar Bill Y'All* on CD for $19 at the Gallery.

I like the community of labels. It's small, humble, not exactly well organized. You meet people in a stumbling, haphazard way, which is refreshing in the age of the targeted ad. Steve at Moon Glyph. Tom at Mirror Universe. Emily at Love Lion. Opal Tapes, Trilogy Tapes, Leaving Records. I usually have not heard of their artists; they do not typically have publicists "working the record." I often buy five or six tapes at a time, whatever releases are available. Sometimes they come right away, other times they take three weeks and two of the cassettes don't have music on them. I listen to cassettes on a small Sony boombox (with Mega Bass), usually when I do the dishes or get ready in the morning. The music feels like a secret between friends.

Certain kinds of music sounds good on cassette. The public perception is that tape is "warm" and "fat," but not all tape is equal, and recording to two-inch tape on an old Studer is very different from playing a cassette in a car stereo. In the cassette heyday, people weren't exactly seeking out cassette releases for their sonic character. Mastering engineers did everything they possibly could to "beat" the cassette into making the music sound pretty damn close to the original recording, despite the ways tape stock can roll off the highs, stuff the low-mids, and hiss above 1 kHz.

I do all my dubbing on old Sony high-speed duplicators, right in my apartment, and I make masters on an old Tascam 112. I don't do a lot of tricks to maintain the high-end frequency response; I like how the music rolls off after 12-15 kHz, sometimes sooner, and can suddenly feel distant and bottom heavy. The drum hits are sanded down, the metals less aggressive. It's a subtle effect. Regardless of encoding the music with Dolby Noise Reduction, I still find that I have to push the mixes a bit to stay above the tape noise. And maybe this is what people are responding to when they say tapes are warm and fat—the sound of music just a little bit more compressed than it should be, as the tape struggles to fit all that information in 1/16 of an inch. This isn't great for atmospheric indie rock. But it's great for punk, noise, hard techno, rap—any kind of music that benefits from sounding loud and unruly and uncontainable.

There's also a metaphysical aspect of cassette releases: the way they affect the musician's performances during recording. I tell my friends I'll record their music and we'll put it out on cassette, and it changes the entire energy of the session. There's less pressure. It's less of an event than a vinyl release. It's *just* a cassette, which is liberating. It lets the id back in the room. There's a feeling of impunity. It's not going to cost anyone too much money. Everybody goes for broke.

Speaking of vinyl, which is an expensive gamble for a small label, I like that cassettes are inexpensive. I buy them in bulk from National Audio Company in Missouri for around 50 cents each,

---

[4] A week after the piece ran, writer Simon Reynolds questioned whether this anti-ideological stance is its own kind of ideology. Replacing one system of meaning for another, basically. To say nothing of the fact that a 'pure response' to music—sound as pure pleasure—is impossible after a certain point. We can't shut off our brains from creating meaning, from bringing former judgments and experiences into the present ones. ¶ It gets trickier because, as others pointed out when I first mentioned my problem with music being enslaved by context—the think-piece era!—there is great pleasure in creating meaning. It's a way of interacting with music. Simon's point combines those two thoughts: That we are all creating meaning on some subconscious level. And my anti-ideology, as worded, encroaches on other people's ability to create said pleasure-meaning. My describing this anti-ideology at length in this published piece further encroaches on how people approach music on cassettes! ¶ Well fuck me, right? Sidestepping "everything about music that isn't music" would mean listening to anonymous untagged audio on the internet and shutting the hell up. ¶ Please pardon my imprecision. I like cassettes because they are removed from the conversation, and aren't bogged down by too much context. ¶ The music I like on cassette falls somewhere between Heavily Contextualized Music and an anonymous internet audio funhouse. And for me, the subdued context of cassettes lets me get back to this very simple fantasy of communion between listener and artist. Call it ideology, or just romance: this idea that the music is a mediator between listener and artist, and from that relationship, that both come out feeling slightly less alone.

and jewel cases are about 22 cents each. Usually I end up doing my own artwork and labels. Runs of 50 or 100 are small by any standard, but if you want to do everything, they take more time than you might think. I don't like the word "cheap" here, but I like the situation that not having to worry about money puts me in. It's just a cassette. I don't feel bad about giving them away to people. Most people I don't expect to even listen; I doubt they have cassette players. But I'm interested in those 10 or 15 people who end up trying. Those 10 or 15 people are more interesting to me than Soundcloud plays.

The sonic resonance of cassettes, the low price point, the performances they inspire, the inevitably rinky-dink machines people end up playing them on—all this amounts to its own kind of musical performance with its own set of expectations. People don't expect perfection from cassettes. They don't expect transparency, or the feeling of being in the room with the band. They might even expect a little bit of distance. I think a lot about Daft Punk's "Revolution 909" in that regard. The music is low-passed for the first minute or so—the thumping and rumbling and undefined sound of standing outside whichever dance club is playing the song inside. The high frequencies are missing, and it creates a longing. This is an extreme example of my point, but psychologically, if you are inundated with clean and clear and sparkly full spectrum digital music all the time, there is something beguiling about music that is happening on the other side of the door.[5] You want to go inside, but you never can.

Notice I have said nothing about having nostalgia for the physical object, or the experience of listening to music on a Walkman, or some Stockholm Syndrome-like "appreciation" for tape hiss. This has nothing to do with making mixtapes either. Emotionally, syntactically, or otherwise, I have never had an issue with the "mix CD." But mixtapes are another extreme version of what I mean by cassettes bearing our stain well. When you make a cassette from scratch—the music, the dubbing, the labels, the art, the liners, even the casing—these little human imperfections accumulate in a way that makes the music mean something different. I can't think of another format that allows for this kind of thing.

I don't think we're in the middle of any long-lasting revival here. It's a lot of work to put out music on cassettes, and to play music on cassettes. For obvious reasons, we value speed and ease and efficiency in our technology, and require a good qualitative reason for deviating. People value the extremes, and cassettes are not extreme. They are about people: 30, 50, 100 or so. Who are they? Why do they want this? How did they find me? I don't psychoanalyze. But I like to think that people who adore cassettes are a little bit like me—they are enormous fans of new music, overwhelmed by the speed and context and game of it all. People who want a community, not a social network. People who want the music, not the meaning. Cassette people, I like to think, want romance and fantasy. A person in a room, making music, putting it in cassette-shaped bottles for no other reason than these cassette-shaped bottles tend to find the people who need their music the most. Total romance and fantasy, all of this, I admit it. But music could use more of both. ✐

Nick Sylvester *is the founder of GODMODE, a Brooklyn-based music company. Currently he is producing the music for "Football For Amateurs", a video game by* The Colbert Report's *Rob Dubbin. He is also designing a delay effect unit based on the Realistic Electronic Reverb circuit.*

---

[5] Allow me one "If I Was Writing This Piece for *Vice*" flourish: It's kind of like how the adult film industry got really weird about HD video. Far from flattering the actors, the crispness of HD revealed all the skin blemishes, the follicles, the human body in its rotting fleshy form. There are any number of illusions involved with the kind of lust that pornography manufactures. But the detail took us out of the dream. So they say! You just got Vice'd!

~~Poop Dreams~~
~~Bathroom Runs (Puns)~~
~~R. Smelly~~

The Infinite Monkey Theorem

They say if you have a roomful of monkeys typing randomly for an infinite amount of time, they will eventually turn out the collected works of Shakespeare. Well, something similar happened in the Pitchfork TV office bathroom. We present and applaud the collective beautiful mind of the Pitchfork TV staff. These Kafkaesque doodles are created in a collaborative process during each staff member's [epic] trips to the toilet. Simultaneously evoking both the ancient cave art of Lascaux and Banksy, modern art has culminated here. Like indulgently proud parents, we are pleased to ~~hang this on our fridge~~ publish their work.

AT OUTDATED ENDEAVOR IS MAKING A COME-BACK WITH TODAY'S NTERPRISING HIPSTER?

HERE WE GO WITH ANOTHER RIDICULOUS
MAD RIP-OFF
More and more people are resurrecting long forgotten practices and pasttimes. Some are worthwhile pursuits, while others are best left alone. To see the latest questionable resurgence among today's top taste-makers, fold page as shown.

FOLD PAGE OVER LIKE THIS!

A   FOLD PAGE OVER LEFT   B   FOLD BACK SO THAT "A" MEETS "B"

THESE DAYS, PEOPLE ARE REACHING FURTHER BACK IN TIME FOR THEIR INTERESTS. IN FACT, SOME NEIGHBORHOODS HAVE BEEN MAGICALLY TRANSPORTED TO A BYGONE TIME. THERE'S SOME AMA-ZING THINGS HAPPENING, BUT HOW LONG IT LASTS, ONLY TIME CAN TELL.

WRITER AND ARTIST: JOHNNY SAMPSON

A   B

CONVERSE RUBBER TRACKS LIVE

is a free concert series featuring headliners who select and perform with up-and-coming artists that have recorded at Converse Rubber Tracks. Pitchfork and Converse are bringing this concept from the stage to the Pitchfork Review. In upcoming issues, some of our favorite artists will co-release a 7-inch split vinyl with emerging musicians that have recorded at Converse Rubber Tracks. To see more of what we are up to visit ConverseMusic.Tumblr.com.

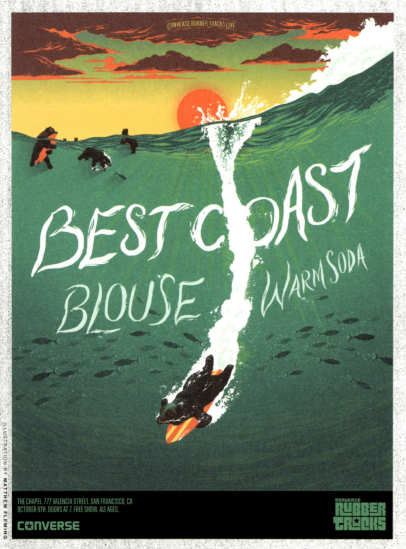

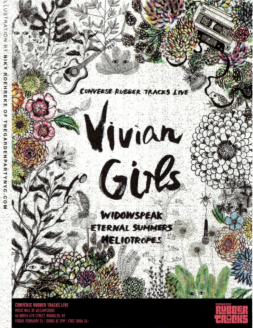